YUU
MIYAZAKI

ILLUSTRATION BY
okiura

THE ASTERISK WAR

11. THE WAY OF THE SWORD

# THE ASTERISK WAR

**11. THE WAY OF THE SWORD**

## YUU MIYAZAKI
### ILLUSTRATION: OKIURA

YEN ON

NEW YORK

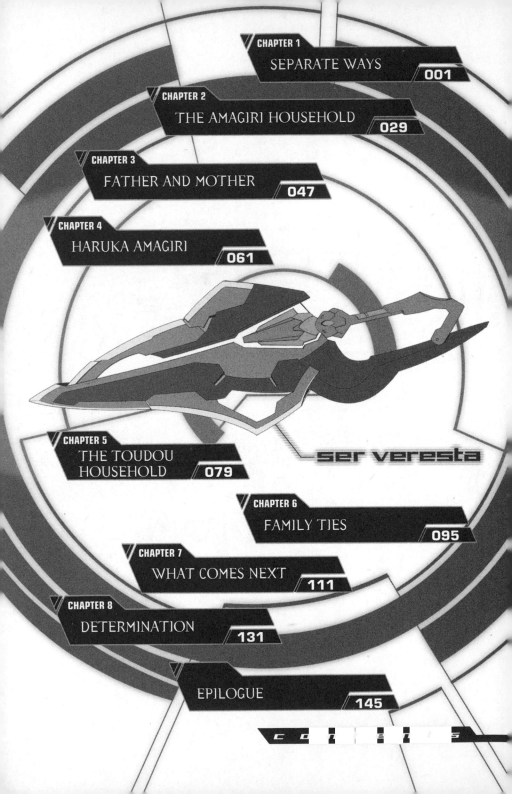

ser veresta

# SEIDOUKAN ACADEMY

## AYATO AMAGIRI

The protagonist of this work. Wielder of the Ser Veresta. Alias Murakumo.

**ALIAS:** Gathering Clouds, Murakumo
**ORGA LUX:** Ser Veresta

## JULIS-ALEXIA VON RIESSFELD

Princess of Lieseltania. Ayato's partner for the Phoenix.

**ALIAS:** the Witch of the Resplendent Flames, Glühen Rose
**LUX:** Aspera Spina

## CLAUDIA ENFIELD

Student council president at Seidoukan Academy. Leader of Team Enfield.

**ALIAS:** the Commander of a Thousand Visions, Parca Morta
**ORGA LUX:** Pan-Dora

## SAYA SASAMIYA

Ayato's childhood friend. An expert in weaponry and machines.

**ALIAS:** none yet given
**LUX:** type 38 Lux grenade launcher Helnekraum, type 34 wave cannon Ark Van Ders Improved Model, and others

## KIRIN TOUDOU

Disciple of the Toudou School of swordsmanship with natural talent. Saya's partner for the Phoenix.

**ALIAS:** the Keen Edged Tempest, Shippuu Jinrai
**LUX:** none (wields the katana Senbakiri)

## EISHIROU YABUKI

Ayato's roommate. Member of the newspaper club.

## LESTER MACPHAIL

Number nine at Seidoukan Academy. Brusque and straightforward but has a deep sense of duty.

## RANDY HOOKE

Lester's partner for the Phoenix.

## KYOUKO YATSUZAKI

Ayato and company's homeroom teacher.

## PREVIOUSLY IN *THE ASTERISK WAR*...

In their semifinal match against Team Yellow Dragon, Kirin's clairvoyance was fully unleashed, and she managed to defeat the legendary Xiaohui Wu, Xinglou's Fan highest disciple. The team proceeded to the championships, but Kirin, reeling from the side effects of overusing her newfound ability, was hospitalized and unable to compete. The team was one member short when they faced off against Saint Gallardworth Academy's Team Lancelot, but Ayato finally managed to unlock the seal placed upon him by his sister, Haruka, turning the match on its head and securing an unprecedented victory.

# characters

THE ASTERISK WAR, Vol. 11
YUU MIYAZAKI

Translation by Haydn Trowell
Cover art by okiura

GAKUSEN TOSHI ASTERISK Vol.11 JINSHIN SESSA
© Yuu Miyazaki 2016
First published in Japan in 2016 by KADOKAWA CORPORATION, Tokyo.
English translation rights arranged with KADOKAWA CORPORATION, Tokyo,
through TUTTLE-MORI AGENCY, INC., Tokyo.

English translation © 2019 by Yen Press, LLC

Yen On
150 West 30th Street, 19th Floor
New York, NY 10001

Visit us at yenpress.com
facebook.com/yenpress
twitter.com/yenpress
yenpress.tumblr.com
instagram.com/yenpress

First Yen On Edition: October 2019

Yen On is an imprint of Yen Press, LLC.
The Yen On name and logo are trademarks of Yen Press, LLC.

Library of Congress Cataloging-in-Publication Data
Names: Miyazaki, Yuu, author. | Tanaka, Melissa, translator. |
Trowell, Haydn, translator.
Title: The asterisk war / Yuu Miyazaki ; translation by Melissa Tanaka.
Other titles: Gakusen toshi asterisk. English
Description: First Yen On edition. | New York, NY : Yen On, 2016– |
v. 6–8 translation by Haydn Trowell | Audience: Ages 13 & up.
Identifiers: LCCN 2016023755 | ISBN 9780316315272 (v. 1 : paperback) |
ISBN 9780316398589 (v. 2 : paperback) | ISBN 9780316398602 (v. 3 : paperback) |
ISBN 9780316398626 (v. 4 : paperback) | ISBN 9780316398657 (v. 5 : paperback) |
ISBN 9780316398671 (v. 6 : paperback) | ISBN 9780316398695 (v. 7 : paperback) |
ISBN 9780316398718 (v. 8 : paperback) | ISBN 9781975302801 (v. 9 : paperback) |
ISBN 9781975329358 (v. 10 : paperback) | ISBN 9781975303518 (v. 11 : paperback)
Subjects: CYAC: Science fiction. | BISAC: FICTION / Science Fiction / Adventure.
Classification: LCC PZ7.1.M635 As 2016 | DDC [Fic]—dc23
LC record available at https://lccn.loc.gov/2016023755

ISBNs: 978-1-9753-0351-8 (paperback)
978-1-9753-0430-0 (ebook)

1  3  5  7  9  10  8  6  4  2

LSC-C

Printed in the United States of America

# CHAPTER 1
# SEPARATE WAYS

It was early winter, the time of year when the cold truly began to seep into one's body.

The five of them—Ayato, Julis, Claudia, Saya, and Kirin—had gathered in the academy's cafeteria as they did every school day.

"Ah, um, everyone!" Kirin began, bowing her head deeply. "Thank you—again!"

It was a little over a month since the Gryps had come to a close. Even Kirin, who had been hospitalized for three days following her injuries in the semifinal, had by now fully recovered. It seemed that her eyes, which had been the group's main cause of concern, would be fine so long as she didn't overuse her newfound clairvoyance ability—the power to read her opponent's movements through sensing the way they channeled their prana.

"...For what?" Julis, having finished her lunch, stared blankly back at her over the lip of her teacup.

"Ah, r-right! I just got word that my father was released the other day..."

"Well now, that *is* cause for celebration!" Claudia clapped once, a warm smile lighting up her face.

Kirin's father, Seijirou, had been imprisoned for killing a thief who had tried to take her hostage many years ago, but it sounded like, thanks to Kirin's long efforts, he had been released without issue.

No matter where you went in the world, if a Genestella ended up hurting an ordinary person, the punishment tended to be much more severe than it would be for anyone else. Under normal circumstances, Seijirou would have had little hope of being released for at least several decades, and yet—

"So, in only a month, his sentence gets reduced thanks to a retrial, and then he gets out thanks to time served... They really do move fast." Saya nodded to herself, as if impressed.

Of course, all that had only happened thanks to the integrated enterprise foundations that had acted on Kirin's behalf after their team had won the Gryps.

"And...he sent this. Please, take a look." Kirin took a carefully folded letter from her pocket, holding it out formally with both hands.

Ayato took it in his own, opening it slowly to reveal the solemnly written, polite words of thanks.

It was a straightforward, simple letter—the kind of message that revealed a genuine, honest character.

"I know it says so right there, but he'd like to thank you all in person too. So...I know this isn't really the same as when Julis invited us all to Lieseltania last year, but if you can make it, I'd be so happy if you could all come and visit us during the winter vacation..."

At that, Ayato and the others each exchanged uncertain looks.

Julis was the first to speak up. "Hmm... I'm grateful, but I'll have to decline," she said, shaking her head sadly. "The Gryps has made me all too aware of just how far I still have to go if I'm going to win the Lindvolus next year. I need to get stronger. Which is why I plan to spend the vacation training."

"Really?" Ayato asked. "Does that mean you're not even going back to Lieseltania?"

"Ah, my brother's keeping me up-to-date on everything. And Flora, too," Julis answered with a somewhat forlorn smile.

Whatever they were telling her, it must have been in relation to her own wish as a champion of the Gryps.

That wish was to greatly expand the authority of the king in order to pull Lieseltania out from under the thumb of the IEFs—but, of course, that wouldn't be an easy feat. At any rate, it would unmistakably be to the disadvantage of the foundations.

Naturally, given that Julis had already publicly announced what she wanted, there was no way they could openly ignore it—that would be against the rules of the Festa. But as with the furor that Claudia had brought down on herself—although strictly speaking, Lieseltania probably wasn't worth as much as Claudia's information—if the loss outweighed the gain, and push came to shove, it wasn't clear how the foundations would react.

As such, Julis's brother, Jolbert, seemed to be working things out behind the scenes. Winners of the Festa had one year to formally request their wish, and Julis intended to spend that time hammering out the details while maintaining a suitable power balance among the various foundations.

"...I'd really like to go as well, but I have something I can't get out of," Saya added regretfully.

"Ah, you mean that Lux development facility that you mentioned?"

"Yes. They're moving it to a new location right around the start of the break. So I should probably be there for it."

Among Asterisk's six schools, only Allekant Académie had formal Lux development facilities. The other schools generally received their Luxes from their parent foundation and only had sufficient equipment to adjust and configure what they were given.

It wasn't as if knowledge of Seidoukan's unofficial facilities had been leaked to the public, but thanks to the school's successful joint development of the new Rect Luxes with Allekant, the decision had been made to come to a more formal arrangement.

Incidentally, Saya, now a member of the Society for the Study of Meteoric Engineering, had already managed to secure herself a factory for her own exclusive use.

"This is still confidential," Claudia began with a chuckle, "but Saya's father, Souichi Sasamiya, is going to take up an expert advisory role at the Matériel Department for the next academic year."

"Huh? Really?"

This was the first that Ayato had heard about it. Nonetheless, given that Souichi had in the past worked with Galaxy's research institution, there was nothing particularly unusual about this turn of events.

"We're planning to set up a direct line with him soon," Saya added with a glowing smile.

For her wish after winning the Gryps, Saya had immediately settled on money.

Her father, Souichi, had lost his body in an accident, and his mind was now integrated into his laboratory in Germany. The maintenance alone required a considerable, continuous supply of funds, and while it wasn't as if the Sasamiyas had been living in need thus far, Saya had no doubt wanted backup resources for whatever the future might bring.

On top of that, Saya was interested in developing her own Luxes, and she seemed to have put some of her newfound capital toward her own uses, too.

"I'm terribly sorry, but my schedule is rather tight for the winter vacation as well...," Claudia said with a bitter smile as she folded her hands together in her lap.

Since the end of the tournament, Claudia seemed to be even busier than usual. Apparently her discussions with Galaxy were picking up pace.

"I—I see... You all sound very busy..." Kirin's shoulders slumped with disappointment.

They each had their own reasons, of course, but she mustn't have been expecting all of them to turn down the invitation.

At that moment, she timidly glanced up at Ayato. She stared at him with almost-tearful, imploring eyes, like those of an abandoned puppy.

"Um, ah, I mean... Ayato...h-how about you?"

Ayato found himself at the center of an indescribable vortex of pressure as everyone silently turned toward him. "I'm sorry, Kirin," he said with a shake of his head. "I have to go home, too... I got a message from my dad. He said he needs to talk about something."

"Oh..." At this response, Kirin closed her eyes, slumping back in her chair. The shock, it seemed, was too much for her to bear.

Ayato was struck by a wave of guilt, but given the situation, there was nothing to be done.

"A message from home...?" Julis asked carefully. "About your sister?"

"Probably. I've got something I need to discuss with him myself, so it's good enough timing, I suppose...," Ayato answered, his mind going back to his meeting with Madiath Mesa the other day.

\*

"Well now, sit down," Madiath Mesa said with an affable smile, as he welcomed Ayato into his office at the Festa Executive Committee headquarters.

A vague sense of nervousness came over Ayato as he took a seat on the sofa. "...All right."

He had already met Madiath face-to-face several times, so he was hardly a stranger, and yet Ayato couldn't help but feel slightly on edge.

"Let's get down to business. Your wish this time is to wake up your sister, correct?"

"Yes."

Madiath, sitting across from him, with his hands folded, leaned forward. "I'll start with our conclusions—the result of our investigations... It seems waking her, in and of itself, is by no means impossible."

"Really?!" Before he knew it, Ayato had begun to rise to his feet in excitement.

Madiath merely looked back at him with a troubled smile. "Stay calm, now. Let me go through everything in order."

"Y-yes, of course... Sorry," Ayato responded as he sat back down.

"Firstly, it goes without saying that the person most knowledge-able about your sister's condition is Director Jan Korbel," Madiath began slowly. "He hasn't been able to find a way to wake her over these past five years, but now that the conditions have changed, you could say that a new possibility has revealed itself—a new form of treatment that he would like to attempt."

"The conditions?"

"If it's to fulfill the wish of one of our Festa champions, the integrated enterprise foundations will support you fully. Whether its funds, facilities, staff, or anything else that you might require, all of it will be put at your disposal."

*Of course.*

Thus far, Director Korbel had been treating her out of his sense of responsibility to help those in need, so there were no doubt limits to the options available to him.

"That said, we're only talking about a possibility here. The Director tells me that this new form of treatment is still only theoretical. Moreover, it sounds like it would probably take quite some time. This is, of course, outside my area of expertise, and I can't claim to understand the details, but it sounds like it involves analyzing the junction pattern of the ability that she set on herself and then dispelling the mana. That would be a time-consuming process, apparently. According to the Director, it would take at least a few years…quite possibly a decade."

"A decade…?!" That was enough to send Ayato, having just gotten his hopes up, flailing once more into the depths of despair.

Of course, it was undeniably good news to hear there was now a chance of waking her, and yet…

"Well… There is another option available to you," Madiath continued, with a faint smile.

"Huh?"

"As it happens, one other individual has stepped forward to offer their assistance."

Ayato knew at once what he was getting at.

"…Magnum Opus, you mean?"

"Oh? She did say her name would suffice to remind you, but it sounds like you didn't even need that." Madiath nodded in admiration. "But yes, I'm talking about Miss Rowlands from Allekant

Académie. She claims that if you fulfill her request, she will be able to wake your sister without delay. And our own investigations suggest she isn't merely boasting."

Ayato cast Madiath a glaring look. "Is it really befitting of the Festa Executive Committee Chairman to consult such a dangerous person?"

Relying on Magnum Opus meant giving her free rein to continue her other pursuits.

Rowlands's so-called research had already swallowed up Julis's childhood friend, Orphelia Landlufen. Ayato couldn't allow another tragedy like that to befall someone else.

"Dangerous...? Ah, you're talking about her experiments? Well..." Madiath stared at him in apparent surprise, before leaning back into his chair as he loosened his collar. "They certainly are rather inhumane. And yet...what's the matter?"

Ayato found himself shuddering at the sudden iciness that had engulfed Madiath's voice and countenance.

"Befitting of the Festa Executive Committee Chairman, you say...? Hah, quite the opposite, Amagiri. It's precisely because I *am* the Executive Committee Chairman that I'm obliged to listen to what she has to say. Just as the winners of the Festa may be granted any wish they desire, so too must we be ready to deal with any possible wish that happens to come our way. You don't honestly think that all our champions are as noble-minded as Miss Riessfeld, interested only in helping others, now, do you? Wealth, fame, women, revenge...people hide all kinds of desires that they would never reveal to the outside world. And we have always done our utmost to grant every last one of them. Of course, there are always those we can't publicly be seen to play a hand in, and, of course, those that are simply impossible to realize. But in the end, it's always a question of degree more than anything else."

"That's..."

There was no arguing that the Festa—or rather, all of Asterisk—was that kind of place, that it existed for that very reason. And it was true that many wishes granted to winners were never made public.

Even Ayato understood that—but only now did it truly feel real to him.

"Don't misunderstand me. We are on *your* side here, not hers. I'm merely pointing out to you, after investigating all your options, what looks to us like the optimal solution. Whichever course of action you choose is up to you."

Madiath's eyes seemed to bore into him, but there was no falsehood in them. Ayato understood that intuitively.

And so Ayato couldn't bring himself to respond.

"I may as well ask about her request... Am I correct in assuming that she wants her penalty revoked? Well, we can always ignore that and simply compel her to assist you. That's always an option. And yet...I would caution against that in your case. I'm sure I don't need to explain why."

"...Because she's the only one with the necessary skills, so success or failure is up to her. Right?"

If they tried to force Magnum Opus to do what they wanted, and it ended in failure, it would all be over. The deal stood only so long as they each had something to gain from it.

"Exactly. You might use the power of the foundations as something of a threat as well. We could set it up so that if she failed, she would never have that penalty of hers withdrawn again, for example... But I'm guessing someone of her disposition wouldn't appreciate that."

"..."

Ayato couldn't bring himself to respond. Those were his thoughts, too.

Hilda Jane Rowlands, better known by the alias Magnum Opus, was the very definition of a mad genius. No matter what kind of pressure was exerted on her, her passions, burning hotter than lava, were unlikely to yield.

Even Ayato, who had only met her once, recognized that.

"Can I... Can I have some time to think about it?"

"Of course. Take your time."

"...Then I'll get going. Excuse me."

But as Ayato made his way toward the exit, Madiath called out from behind. "Remember, whichever course of action you decide on, we'll do our utmost to make it happen. Keep that in mind."

*

"Like I said a while back," Julis began, her expression serious, "I won't blame you, no matter what you do. Not even if you decide to go with Magnum Opus."

"I know. Thanks, Julis," Ayato replied with a forced smile, before turning back to Kirin. "So…I'm really sorry, Kirin."

"Th-there's no need to apologize, Ayato…!" she responded, shaking her hands vehemently. It was clear enough from her expression, however, that she was disappointed.

*I should probably send Seijirou a letter at least, to thank him for the invitation…*

"Kirin," Saya said from her spot beside her, "even though we can't make it this time, I'm going to visit soon, even if you change your mind and say not to." She patted her on the shoulder. "So don't worry."

"…Even if she doesn't want you to, Saya?" Claudia said softly, her voice dubious. "But Kirin, do invite us again, as friends. There's no need for your father to go out of his way to thank us."

"Huh? B-but it's thanks to you all that we won the Gryps…"

"You were part of that victory, Kirin. We couldn't have done it without you," Julis corrected with a gentle smile as she stroked her friend's head.

"B-but I wasn't there, not when you needed me the most, in the final…"

"If that's how you want to put it, then *we* should be thanking *you*. If you hadn't taken down Hagun Seikun in the semifinal, we would have never even made it to the championship."

"Th-that's…!" Kirin's face reddened. She stared down at the table.

"Ha-ha, but Julis is right." Ayato grinned. "The Gryps might be over, but we're still a team, and we're all still friends. It's only natural for us to count on one another, right?"

"Y-yes!" Kirin nodded forcefully, her eyes brimming with tears. And yet—

"Well then, now that Ayato has brought that topic to a wonderful close...I'd like to speak to you all about next year's individual tournament, where we may end up fighting one another." With this, Claudia put her hands together with an adorable clap, tilting her head slightly.

"Claudia, you..."

"...You've spoiled the mood."

Julis and Saya narrowed their eyes at her, but Claudia continued to smile, showing no concern whatsoever for their sharp gazes.

"Unfortunately, as student council president, this is a serious matter that I need to confirm. After all, if either Ayato or Julis were to win at the Lindvolus, they would be the first individual since the second Ban'yuu Tenra to achieve a grand slam."

Gaining consecutive victories in all three Festas in a given season was commonly known as a grand slam, and only one person in all of Asterisk's history had managed to accomplish that feat. Looking at it objectively, there was no mistaking the potential for one of them to achieve something historic.

"Thanks to everyone's efforts, our academy already has a huge advantage in overall points. Although I suppose that goes without saying, considering we won both the Phoenix and the Gryps. Even if we lose at the Lindvolus, there's still a high possibility that we would come out on top as far as points are concerned. However, now that we've come this far, I'm quite sure that Galaxy would prefer that we—"

"—go all the way," Saya finished for her.

Claudia nodded. "Indeed... But so long as the reigning champion is around, I'm afraid that will be rather difficult."

"Don't worry. I'll take care of Orphelia." Julis's voice was quiet, but there was no mistaking the iron force of will that rang through it.

"I thought you would say that, Julis," Claudia said with a chuckle. "But even so..."

"You don't need to worry about that," Ayato said as he met her gaze. "I won't be participating. I don't want to get in Julis's way."

"Indeed… I *thought* you would say that." Claudia's shoulders slumped.

Julis, meanwhile, seemed to be blushing slightly, her eyes refusing to meet his. "Y-you don't need to worry about me, or anything, all right? Even if we were to face each other, I'd just take you head-on and beat you to a pulp."

"Ha-ha… But now that I've got a better grasp of Haruka's situation, I don't really need to enter it anymore. I don't have any other wishes that need granting."

His original reason for taking part in the Festa was to help Julis, to be her strength. Even if through that he had managed to locate his sister and now hoped to finally wake her, he wasn't about to abandon Julis.

And he would be much freer to support her outside the tournament. Various troubles had reared their heads during both the Phoenix and the Gryps, after all, and there was no guarantee that something similar wouldn't happen during the Lindvolus.

"You're as selfless as ever, I see… What about you, Saya?" Claudia asked.

"I'll be in it," Saya answered with a short nod. "I've got a score to settle."

That score was no doubt with Camilla Pareto of Allekant…or rather, with her puppets, Ardy and Rimcy. Saya and Camilla's relationship seemed to have developed into something of a rivalry since the end of the Phoenix.

"But if all you want to do is settle a score, wouldn't a duel be enough…?" Kirin asked, her voice tinged with curiosity.

Saya let out a slight sigh, shaking her head. "I agree… But Ardy and Rimcy belong to Ferrovius and Pygmalion, so Camilla Pareto can't just use them as she pleases."

"Well, they probably wouldn't come out of it in one piece if they went against you, right?" Ayato joked.

Camilla's position at Allekant seemed to be rather secure, but even so, there would almost certainly be consequences for her should either of the two puppets be damaged while using them to settle a private matter.

"It sounds like she's planning on entering, and this time victory will be mine." Saya was working herself up, clenching her fists tightly. "So if I'm put against you, Julis, I'm not going to go easy. I'll knock you out stone cold."

"Hmph. That's my line. I'll roast you along with all your Luxes."

Claudia watched from the side as the two of the them glared at each other ferociously, before she let out a feigned cough and turned to her next target. "Ahem. Well then, Kirin. What about you?"

"Ah... I—I, I mean... I haven't decided yet..." Kirin spoke evasively, averting her gaze as if trying to hide.

Kirin tended to look rather timid at first glance. This time, however, Ayato found himself struck by a vague sense of discomfort.

She may well have been rather reserved with regard to pretty much anything that wasn't related to her mastery of the sword, but she wasn't the kind of person to be paralyzed by indecision. And yet, right now, she clearly seemed to be of two minds.

"Hmm, I see," Claudia answered with a light chuckle. "There's no need to worry about it yet. After all, it isn't for close to a year. Please, think it over carefully before you make your decision. Although... there's no denying that, as far as the school is concerned, we would prefer you take a break this time."

"Huh?"

"...What's that supposed to mean?" At this, Julis—who, until that very moment, had still been butting heads with Saya—turned her piercing gaze toward Claudia. "This better not have anything to do with anyone getting in the way of me scoring a grand slam. If it does—"

"No, of course not. Kirin has already taken part in two Festas, you see. Taking into account her age, and the fact that she still has plenty of room to grow, it would be a waste to have her use her third and final opportunity now, wouldn't you say?"

"That's..." Julis, no doubt realizing there was nothing wrong with Claudia's reasoning, held her tongue.

No student in Asterisk could participate in the Festa more than three times. That was one of the fundamental rules set out in the Stella Carta. There was no denying it would be regrettable for Kirin to use up all her opportunities while still only a middle school student.

As far as Ayato was concerned, her skill with a sword was already a cut above his own.

It wasn't hard to believe that, one day soon, she might even surpass Saint Gallardworth Academy's former student council president Ernest Fairclough.

"Which is *why...*" All of a sudden, Claudia's voice became bright and buoyant. "We would like you to consider this." She opened an air-window, sending it toward Kirin.

Projected in the middle of it was—

"...A katana?"

"No. If you look carefully, it's got a small core. It's a Lux... No, wait a second. It's..."

Julis and Saya, having crowded behind Kirin to get a better look, couldn't help but murmur their impressions.

"Very good, Saya. You clearly have an eye for these things. Yes, it's a very intriguing katana-shaped Orga Lux, and with an intriguing name, too. The Fudaraku. It's written with the characters for *lotus* and *degeneration*, but it's named after the abode of the goddess Kannon."

"An Orga Lux...!"

Claudia nodded, and the remaining four of them swallowed their breath, taken aback more by the sight of the weapon than the explanation of its name.

"Is this that new Orga Lux you said that Galaxy was developing?"

"My, I didn't think you would remember, Ayato."

He remembered her saying something to Kirin along those lines back around the time of the Phoenix.

"Indeed, this is a brand-new item straight from Galaxy. So what do you say, Kirin? Won't you try it?"

"M-me...?"

"Of course, you would need to take a compatibility test first. While you may be unranked right now, I doubt anyone would complain about giving you priority considering your achievements."

"Um, I mean…" Once more, Kirin's expression clouded over.

*Kirin…?*

There was a clear look of hesitation in her eyes.

*Something* was bothering her.

"We won't force you. But with your Senbakiri beyond repair, you're going to need a replacement, don't you think?"

Amid the ferocity of their semifinal match in the Gryps, Kirin's cherished Senbakiri had been shattered. As a result, she had been using a standard blade-type Lux for the past few weeks.

Additionally, Ayato's Ser Veresta had been destroyed in the championship match.

While his Orga Lux could at least be repaired, restoring it to its previous condition, and, of course, adjusting it to his own requirements, would probably take several months.

For that reason, Ayato was also making do with his spare blade-type Lux.

To make matters worse, even once the Ser Veresta's repairs were complete, it wasn't at all certain that it would still allow him to wield it. That possibility was what had Ayato most concerned.

"But what does giving Kirin this Orga Lux have to do with her not participating in the Festa?" Julis asked bluntly.

If the Fudaraku truly was powerful, it would have made more sense from the school's perspective to give it to someone else if Kirin wasn't going to take part in the upcoming Festa.

"Well, the Fudaraku's ability is somewhat…or shall I say, *fairly* special, you see," Claudia answered with an impish grin. "However… Well, I can explain everything in detail later. Please, just keep it in mind."

"…Why? You don't need to put on airs." Saya pouted.

Claudia, however, merely glanced at her watch with an elegant flourish. "I'm afraid that we're out of time."

At that very moment, the school bell rang out, signaling the end of their midday lunch break.

"Argh, already?" Saya grumbled.

With that, as they each stood up from their seats, Claudia put her hands together giddily and approached Ayato, as if only now remembering something important.

"I'll be waiting for you at the hotel after class," she whispered into his ear.

"…Huh?"

When Ayato, who had turned stiff for a moment with a rush of confusion, turned around, Claudia was already making her way toward the exit, her expression as composed as ever.

"W-wait, Claudia…!"

He called after her, only to have his mobile ring with an incoming message.

It contained only two things: a meeting time and a room number at the Hotel Elnath.

*

The Elnath was Asterisk's foremost luxury hotel, renowned for the gardens on its top floor, which served as the meeting place of the monthly Rikka Garden Summit, where the student council presidents of Asterisk's six schools exchanged opinions with and attempted to outmaneuver their counterparts.

Ayato had come alone to a room in that very high-rise building. As he inserted the key card he had been given at reception into the slot by the indicated room, the door swung open without a sound.

Waiting for him amid the darkness was—

"Ayato! It's been a while!"

"Sylvie…?!"

Sylvia, lounging on the sofa inside, waved to him with a delighted smile.

"Sylvie, what are you doing here…?"

"What am I doing…? You haven't heard?"

"Ah, not really. A few minutes ago, Claudia told me to come here, so here I am…"

At that moment, Claudia appeared from the back of the room, grasping a glass in one hand and a bottle of some kind of beverage in the other.

"My apologies." She chuckled. "I only wanted to tell you the bare minimum, for the sake of security."

"Oh?" Sylvia asked, eyeing him suspiciously. "Then were you expecting to get up to something naughty, Ayato?"

"No!" Ayato hurriedly denied. "I just thought that if Claudia was going to go to these extremes, it had to be something really important!"

"My... Thank you for trusting me." But Claudia couldn't keep a faint blush from rising to her cheeks.

"Hmm, I guess Ayato trusts you, Claudia. How lucky for you," Sylvia ribbed, both physically and metaphorically.

"The same goes for you, too, Sylvie. I trust you as well," Ayato hastily amended.

"Huh? R-really?" At this admission, Sylvia's trembling voice was unnaturally high.

Claudia laughed. "It looks like Ayato is quite skilled at taking us by surprise, wouldn't you say?"

"You got me..." Sylvia murmured, hanging her head.

This time, Claudia rested a hand on her shoulder.

"...Are you always like this, Claudia? You don't think you're being unfair?"

"Not at all. I'm sure you'll forgive me this small pleasure. It must pale in comparison to that of being the world's favorite diva."

"Um... So, who are we waiting for?" Ayato asked nervously, interrupting their banter.

Claudia had prepared four glasses. In other words, there was still one more person yet to arrive.

"That would be... Ah, what impeccable timing."

As Claudia spoke, Ayato—and, of course, Sylvia too—noticed someone else approaching.

"...It looks like everyone's here."

The voice belonged to a black-suited figure with long, blonde hair.

The second Ayato laid eyes on that gentle smile, Ayato knew

exactly who she was. Her face and mannerisms were too much like Claudia's.

"How do you do, Ayato Amagiri? And you, Sylvia Lyyneheym? My name is Isabella Enfield."

*Of course.*

"It seems my daughter is indebted to you especially, Amagiri."

"N-no, I just..."

Standing in front of him was the very woman who had put Claudia's—no, her own daughter's—life in such jeopardy during the Gryps.

Looking at her now, Ayato could hardly believe her capable of such a thing.

"Now then, we're pressed for time, so let's get right to it, shall we? After all, we've gone to the trouble of having not only an incredibly busy top IEF executive, but also the world's most popular idol, give us some of their precious time," Claudia began as the four of them took their seats at the nearby table.

"So... What's going on?" Even Ayato could tell this kind of meeting wasn't a normal occurrence.

Isabella was the CEO of the foundation Galaxy, while Sylvia was the student council president of Queenvale Academy for Young Ladies, whose parent company was W&W. Sylvia was undoubtedly crossing a very dangerous line simply by being here.

"I told you earlier, before the championship match at the Gryps, that there was something I wanted to discuss with you, right?" Sylvia began.

"Sure, but why do we need—"

"Because she's heavily involved in it."

"...!"

In other words, this was going to be about—

"Right. We've come to talk about Varda and Lamina Mortis... About the Golden Bough Alliance, basically."

"The Golden Bough Alliance...?"

This was the first time Ayato had heard the name.

"Before we get to that, I probably need to explain some things.

Ayato, I've already told you part of this... The cost of my wielding the Pan-Dora is that I experience my death countless times over, but as a side effect of that, I'm able to piece together bits of information about the past that I wouldn't otherwise have access to."

Ayato stared back at her blankly. "Sorry, what does that have to do with this?" he asked, wishing she would go into a little more depth.

Claudia cupped her chin in her hand, as if deep in thought. "Yes, well... Let's say that my little darling shows me my possible death ten years from now. There's a lot that could change in ten years' time, so that won't be of much use to me. But there may well be tidbits contained within that dream that relate to now, or even to the past—things that most definitely have happened."

"I see... But I thought your dreams mostly faded away when you wake up?"

"Indeed, they do. Which is why my knowledge is only fragmentary at best."

"...Even so, this child knows things that she shouldn't possibly be able to know," Isabella said, following on from her daughter. "You can think of that as being of particular value to us at Galaxy."

Based on their way of speaking, Ayato could guess where this was going.

"Yes, it's as you've no doubt guessed. Galaxy has agreed to let me off for that little incident so long as I provide them with this kind of information," Claudia said in response to his unasked question, her shoulders trembling with amusement.

This time, it was Sylvia's turn to ask: "So, you heard something about the Golden Bough Alliance, then?"

"Before I answer that... You'll have to make a decision," Claudia said, glancing toward Isabella.

"As Claudia just said, this information belongs to Galaxy. Under any normal circumstances, we would never let it fall into the hands of an outsider...let alone the student council president of another school."

"Of course not."

"However... Right now, there probably isn't anyone in Asterisk who has come closer to this Golden Bough Alliance and their members than you. Which is, of course, why W&W are opposed to you having anything further to do with this matter...perhaps why they've chosen to take a neutral position regarding it. That's how it seems to us."

"Well, that isn't a bad guess, I suppose."

Throughout their exchange, neither Isabella nor Sylvia allowed their composed smiles to falter, but it was clear enough that there was an air of tension simmering beneath the surface. They were no doubt trying to probe each other's weaknesses.

"...Very well. In any event, assuming that your ultimate goal is to capture Varda, then our interests are aligned. We're ready to build a cooperative relationship with you. Of course, this would remain secret from both Queenvale and W&W."

"In other words, you want me to join Galaxy?"

"That isn't what we're offering. This offer isn't for Sylvia Lyyneheym, Queenvale's student council president and a globally popular diva; it's for Sylvia Lyyneheym, student and friend of Ursula Svend."

"—!" At the sound of that name, Sylvia's amicable countenance completely vanished. "I see... Yes... Very well. I'm listening."

"I'll say this once more, just in case. If anything about this falls into anyone else's hands, W&W's especially, we won't look very kindly on it, irrespective of whether or not you were to blame. That being the case—"

"All right, I understand," Sylvia interrupted. "Tell me about Varda."

Sylvia was beginning to let her emotions show. At this rate, it was Isabella who would be in control of the discussion. Her forceful personality was, it seemed, a step above.

"Very well. In that case, Claudia?"

"First of all, the thing that you called Varda...is an Orga Lux known as the Varda-Vaos, created by Professor Ladislav Bartošik. Its ability is mental interference...tampering with people's memories and their sense of recognition."

"And the cost of using it is that you lose control over your body, right?"

"My, how impressive, Ayato. So you noticed that, did you?"

Having encountered it in person, both Ayato and Sylvia had already been able to surmise some of the details.

"So, this Orga Lux, this Varda-Vaos—you're saying that it's controlling Ursula's body all by itself?"

It was widely known that Orga Luxes possessed something similar to a sense of will—Ayato himself had felt as much from the Ser Veresta on numerous occasions. But even so, it was only natural to have doubts about the extent of their sense of selfhood.

"Indeed. The first person to fall victim to it was its creator, Professor Bartošik himself. And then…it used its ability to brainwash countless students, and brought about the Jade Twilight Incident."

"—!" Ayato gasped at this new revelation. He knew, of course, that Ladislav was the ideological mastermind behind the Jade Twilight Incident, but this was the first time he was hearing that it had all been due to Varda's manipulation.

What Claudia was describing was on a completely different level.

He found himself shuddering. Sylvia, when he checked, was having a similar reaction.

"You both have a remarkable sense of discernment," Isabella said, nodding.

"…I'm starting to understand why you pushed Galaxy so far, Claudia," Ayato murmured.

"Yes. And now, Galaxy has come to me with a proposal."

The general public had been led to think of the Jade Twilight Incident as an attempt by a group of Genestella supremacists to expand their rights. If, however, the Varda-Vaos could produce terrorists of that kind, it would be capable of bringing about destruction on a global scale.

Moreover, if the world knew that it was Galaxy that had set such a calamity loose, the damage that would do to the organization would be immeasurable. It could very possibly mean the end of Galaxy itself. Not even the integrated enterprise foundations were immortal. After all, there had once been eight, but now they were down to six.

"I hope you understand the risks involved just in telling you all this?" Isabella said with a sigh.

"It seems that Varda found Ursula Svend after going through several different users. I'm afraid I don't know the particulars... but Ayato's report a while back, that it was working with Lamina Mortis, well...that was enough to instill a sense of crisis at Galaxy, it seems... Isn't that right, Mother?"

"Indeed. I've heard a little about this Lamina Mortis myself. He was an executioner who often participated in the Eclipse. Although, even I was surprised to hear that he's still holding onto the Raksha-Nada..."

"Right! That Orga Lux is supposed to belong to Le Wolfe, right?" Ayato asked. "But I thought it was sealed away... So why does he...?"

Isabella slowly shook her head. "He's had it since his time at the Eclipse. Danilo belonged to Solnage, so he must have worked something out behind the scenes."

Danilo Bertoni—the previous Festa Executive Committee Chairman, and the likely mastermind behind the illegal tournament.

Ayato had heard about him from Helga Lindwall.

"Now that you mention it, the commander of the city guard did say there was a possibility that Danilo was being manipulated by some kind of mind control..."

"Right! And when Petra told me about Lamina Mortis—I wondered how he was able to hide his identity with nothing but a mask..."

There could only be one possible conclusion:

"Indeed, it's very likely he was working with Varda even then."

No one would have been able to reach this conclusion without knowing about the Orga Lux's ability.

"Moreover, our intelligence networks have recently heard mention of this Golden Bough Alliance organization's activities here in Rikka. While they haven't been able to learn anything specific, it does seem that Lamina Mortis is involved with them. Which means, of course, that—"

"—Varda is part of it, too," Sylvia murmured, clenching her hands tightly.

"The Golden Bough Alliance seems to have caused little real harm yet, so the foundations have had no reason to set about taking care of them in earnest. The only ones who appear particularly concerned are Galaxy...and Queenvale. Apparently Benetnasch has lost several operatives."

"Yes... I heard about that," Sylvia said pointedly.

Isabella met her gaze with an impenetrable smile. "However, because of that, we can't make any large-scale moves by ourselves. If Galaxy was to mobilize its own units, the other foundations would soon catch wind, exactly as they did last time. That wouldn't be good. It would risk tipping off Varda, Lamina Mortis, and any of their associates. When we do make a move, it has to be with the utmost secrecy."

"...That's where I come in, then?"

"More like, that's where *we* come in, Sylvie," Ayato added.

Sylvia startled, turning toward him. For a long moment, her expression remained grave, but it eventually relented. "Right. Thanks, Ayato."

"As far as I'm concerned, it was Lamina Mortis who did that to Haruka... But I still don't know why he attacked me during the tournament."

Now that he thought back on it, it was almost as if Lamina Mortis had only meant to engage in a practice duel.

Ayato just couldn't understand it.

"We'll keep looking into what he wants with *you*, Ayato, as well," Claudia continued. "But we need to prioritize working out this Golden Bough Alliance's objectives. Everything else depends on that."

Ayato and Sylvia exchanged nods.

"We will not contact you directly after this meeting. You should communicate and share information through Amagiri. And do not trust your communication networks—you will discuss this matter only in person. Sinodomius's information gathering resources in particular are both thorough and extensive." With that, Isabella rose to her feet, before turning her gaze toward Claudia. "We have another engagement, so we're going to have to leave things there. Let's go, Claudia."

"Ah, Ayato, Sylvia. I'm sure you know this, but please make sure that you both leave separately," Claudia added on her way out.

After the two Enfields had departed, Sylvia and Ayato both let out long, weary sighs.

"That was exhausting..." Sylvia yawned. "I'm not good with these IEF higher-ups..."

"Claudia really is a lot like her mother... But it looks like we're well and truly caught up in the middle of things now. Are you really okay with this, Sylvie?"

It was complicated enough for Ayato, but Sylvia had essentially made a secret agreement with a foundation in charge of a rival school. Not only that, but the contents of that agreement were on an entirely different scale than the kinds of things that she had been involved in up till now.

"Thanks for worrying about me, Ayato. But if it helps me save Ursula, then I'm okay with it." She flashed him a firm smile. "Anyway, it's been a while since we've been alone together like this."

"Ah, now that you mention it..."

He had spoken to her briefly after the opening ceremony of the Gryps, but since then, they had communicated only through air-windows.

"He-he... We don't get many chances like this, do we now?" She narrowed her eyes like a cat, carefully drawing closer to him on the sofa.

"Um... Sylvie?"

"You should let me congratulate you properly, Ayato, for winning the Gryps. You were so cool in the final. You made me fall in love with you all over again."

"Ha-ha... It wasn't the most dignified of matches, though."

He had had to get down into the mud in his fierce duel against

Ernest, and it had come to the verge of a bloodletting by the time the match reached its end.

Everyone had their own tastes when it came to battles, but Sylvia was the kind of person who preferred to fight with style and technique—in other words, the exact opposite of how the championship had played out. At the very least, she couldn't have found it particularly pleasant to watch. And yet—

"Not at all! I mean, sure, my heart must have skipped a few beats watching it, but you were amazing. I think you impressed Ernest as well," Sylvia replied, smiling up at him as her face drew still closer to his own. "How are your injuries? Have they all healed by now?"

"Ah, th-they're okay! They're okay, so, um, Sylvie...!"

Her face continued to approach his own, coming keenly, dangerously close, when—

"My apologies," came Claudia's voice out of nowhere. "I'm afraid I left something behind."

At this sudden entrance, Sylvia lost her balance, tumbling forward.

"Oh my, are you all right, Sylvia? You need to take better care of yourself—as a world-renowned songstress of course."

"...Thank you for your concern." The expression on Sylvia's upturned face, however, was the very opposite of gratitude.

"But do you really have time to take things so easily? I was under the impression that you had to weave this meeting into your busy schedule?"

"You look like the one with plenty of time on your hands, coming back here to look for something that may not even exist."

"Ah-hee-hee..."

"Hee-hee-hee..."

Ayato could do little but let out an awkward chuckle as the two of them glared at each other over their perfect smiles.

\*

"...Sorry to keep you waiting, Mother," Claudia said when she returned to the car.

Isabella responded without glancing up from the digital documents that she was looking over. "Did you find what you were looking for?"

"Yes, it was right where I thought it would be."

"Excellent... But for a daughter of mine, you can be rather petty, wouldn't you say?"

"I don't know whether or not I should take that as a compliment," Claudia responded with a light laugh.

She took her seat next to her mother in the rear of the car as it took off, before opening an air-window to take care of her own work.

"Ah, by the way, about that incident..."

"The board of executives has given their permission. Fortunately, they put great stock in the information you provided. They have decided to have me serve as your watchdog, so to speak."

"Oh my. Is that a problem?"

"To be perfectly frank, it's a nuisance, having my time taken up by your personal fancies... What on earth kind of business could you have with Professor Bartošik?"

Yes, Claudia had convinced Galaxy to allow her to speak directly with the detained former professor Ladislav Bartošik.

But not as her wish for being part of the winning team at the Gryps. She was simply in a position to meet him without having to rely on means like that now.

In fact, she had yet to even request a wish. It wasn't that she hadn't thought about what she wanted, but she intended to wait right up until the deadline.

"It might help me gain a better understanding of the Pan-Dora and increase the accuracy of my information. So thank you for your assistance, Mother."

"Hmm..." Isabella let out a deep sigh before returning to her documents.

The information that Claudia had provided Galaxy seemed to have turned out to be remarkably profitable for the foundation. So long as she could keep feeding them more, not even Isabella would complain too much.

And she, after all, was essentially the highest executive at Galaxy. *But will the professor answer my questions...?*

As she watched the evening scenery flow past the window, Claudia gently stroked the activation body of the Orga Lux with which she would share her fate.

# CHAPTER 2
# THE AMAGIRI
# HOUSEHOLD

The wintry wind blowing off the surface of the lake cut deep into his flesh.

For a brief second, Ayato was reminded of the distant nation that he had visited exactly one year earlier.

There had been a great lake in that snow-covered country, too, and the cold air blowing off the water there had been enough to make him want to curl up with a blanket.

"I can't help but think about Lieseltania," Kirin said from his side. Apparently, she was thinking the same thing.

They were standing on the deck of the ferry linking Asterisk to the city on the far shore of the lake.

Behind them, the needlelike high-rise buildings that comprised Asterisk were already fading into the distance.

Ahead of them, on the other hand, waited the lakeside city that essentially served as Asterisk's front door. There was a high-speed railway station there, which both Ayato and Kirin would use to return to their respective homes.

"Well, it's still a bit warmer here, though."

The wind was undeniably frigid, but the sunlight pouring down from the clear, blue skies made up for it somewhat.

Even so, there was hardly anyone else on the deck. Given that it was the end of the year, there was a considerable number of students making their way home, but most, it seemed, were unwilling to needlessly venture outside during the depths of winter.

"...I suppose so." Kirin, wrapping herself tightly in her thick coat, let out a weak laugh, but beneath her feigned smile was more than a touch of somberness. Her tone of voice was unusually low as well.

"Kirin... Is everything okay?"

"Huh...?"

"I mean, you've been looking a bit down since before we left."

Or rather, since she had brought up the letter from her father, Seijirou.

No, now that he thought about it, she seemed to have had something on her mind ever since their victory at the Gryps, often letting out what sounded like tired sighs, or looking uncharacteristically sullen.

"You can always talk to me, if something's bothering you. If you're comfortable discussing it with me, I mean..."

"No, that isn't..." Kirin glanced around furtively for a long moment, before finally letting out a resigned sigh and turning to face him. "I know it's a bit late for this, but the truth is...I'm afraid to go back there."

"Afraid?"

That wasn't the kind of answer that he had been expecting.

"But you'll be able to see your father again for the first time in years, right?"

Ayato knew how much she had been longing to see him.

"Yes, of course, I can't wait to see him, but..."

"But?" Ayato repeated.

Kirin paused for a moment before answering. "It's my great-aunt. I'm a bit uneasy about... I mean..."

"Your great-aunt...? Ah, the one in charge of the Toudou style's head school? Is she difficult to deal with?"

Based on what he had heard previously, she had returned to the head family from one of its many branch schools after what had happened to Kirin's father.

The only one of Kirin's relatives with whom Ayato was acquainted was her uncle Kouichirou. He couldn't help but wonder whether her great-aunt was as self-interested as he was.

"N-no! I mean, she's a wonderful person, really. I respect her a lot!" Kirin cried out to correct him.

There could be no doubting the sincerity that shone in her eyes.

"Then why...?"

"I mean... She's a very perceptive, very disciplined person... She'll just be disappointed if she sees me like I am now..."

"Disappointed...? I don't think so. You've grown tremendously since we first met. The results speak for themselves."

"I'm grateful to hear you say that, Ayato, but still... That isn't really it." Kirin hung her head, biting at her lip. "The real problem is me—with my spirit, I suppose."

"Your spirit...?"

"At the end of the Gryps, I got a call from her. She wanted to congratulate me on our victory, and she asked me to come home to take her place as head of the family."

"...What?!" Ayato's eyes opened wide in surprise.

In other words, she would have to leave Seidoukan.

"My great-aunt was only ever temporarily in charge, and since they won't let my dad take over again..."

"But Kirin...is that what *you* want?"

"N-no! I want to stay at Seidoukan, and—and keep improving my skills with you and the others!"

"I'm glad to hear that."

Her answer came as a relief, and yet—

"But you know... I only went to Asterisk to help my father. Now that I've done that, I don't know whether I can convince her to let me stay..." Her expression darkening, Kirin's voice gradually trailed off.

"She'll understand if you talk it over with her, right...?"

If she was worthy of Kirin's respect, then there was high chance she was the type of person who listened to others' perspectives.

"Maybe she would, normally... But I'm sure she'll see right through me, see just how lost I am..."

"How lost you are?" Ayato wondered.

Kirin raised her head, casting her gaze across the water toward the receding city. "In the way of the sword," she whispered softly.

"..."

Kirin's words rang heavy, and while Ayato wracked his brain for a suitable response, nothing came to mind.

As far as his own swordsmanship was concerned, he too had a long way to go.

"I put everything I had into the semifinal, of course, and I can't say I'm unhappy with the result. But it was due to luck more than anything else that I beat Hagun Seikun."

There was no denying that Hagun Seikun had been a formidable opponent. It was thanks to Kirin's clairvoyance ability that they had won, but even Ayato didn't know whether she would be able to come out on top were she to face him again.

"But still... In spite of that, it's frustrating. I want to become stronger. But I don't know what to do... Like I said, I don't want to leave Seidoukan. It's only thanks to you, Ayato, and the others too, that I've been able to improve like I have. And yet...if I wanted to really master the Toudou style, there's no doubt that it would be best to go home..."

"So...is that why you didn't want to make a decision about the Fudaraku?"

Kirin nodded.

Claudia had first suggested that Kirin try the katana-shaped Orga Lux several days prior. It seemed that, after that first discussion, she had explained its abilities to Kirin in more detail and suggested that she take a compatibility test, but in the end, Kirin had simply asked for more time to think it over.

Personally, to Ayato at least, the Fudaraku's abilities seemed well-suited to her particular battle style, so he had been somewhat surprised by her response.

"That's one option, to start using an Orga Lux... Like Tenka Musou did. But I don't know whether it's the best one..."

Hufeng Zhao, alias Tenka Musou, had used an Orga Lux in that same semifinal match against Xiaohui Wu; he had called it proof of his own weakness, of his shallow fixation on victory.

There was a purity in that way of thinking, but whether or not it had anything to do with the strength Kirin sought was another matter entirely.

"...I don't know what I should do anymore...," Kirin murmured as she tried to stop the wind from blowing her hair into disarray.

Her voice was almost drowned out by an announcement informing them that they would be arriving at the terminal momentarily.

At that, Kirin turned to Ayato, as if only now coming back to her senses, and bowed her head deeply. "I—I'm sorry! This must sound so strange...!"

Ayato's chest ached at the sight of her brave smile.

He understood how important her swordsmanship was to her. It was, in a certain sense, the very core of Kirin Toudou. Ayato could only imagine how uneasy she would have to be to let her trepidation show through her usually unassuming, reserved demeanor.

"...By the way, Kirin," Ayato began. "Did you tell your family when exactly you would be going home?"

"Huh? No, just that I'd be coming back during winter vacation..." Her voice, as she answered him, was frank, though her expression was quizzical.

*I might not be very good at giving advice, but* he *might be...*

Although, to be honest, Ayato didn't like having to rely on him like this.

Still, he couldn't leave Kirin by herself while she had so much on her mind, and he could hardly think of anyone more appropriate to offer guidance of this sort. And above all, if he let this chance slip by, there might not be another.

In that case—

"I-if you're okay with it…how about you come back to my place first?"

"…Huh?" Kirin squeaked, her mouth agape.

Ayato tried to explain. "I mean, my dad might be able to—"

"Huuuuuuuuuuuh?!"

Kirin, however, let out a loud cry before he could finish speaking, her face having turned scarlet.

\*

More than a hundred small flames flickered throughout the darkened training room reserved for Seidoukan Academy's Page Ones.

Each was around the size of a candle, but they had been carefully arranged to sketch out complicated, geometric patterns that continuously shifted in form.

Julis, standing at the center of it all with her eyes tightly shut, focused her prana and concentration to their limits, like an ascetic deep in prayer. The sizes, speed, and timing were precisely as she was imaging them—even the slightest inaccuracy would bring it all crashing down.

Several minutes had passed since she had begun.

When the alarm she had set finally sounded, she opened her eyes and let out a deep sigh.

"Phew… I guess this is it…"

The candles all vanished as the training room's usual floodlights reactivated.

It was Sister Therese from the orphanage in Lieseltania who had first taught her how to do this.

It was a basic form of training for Stregas, essential if one wished to hone one's control over one's prana. When she had first started, she hadn't been able to maintain four such flames for five minutes. When she looked back on it, even she had to admit she had grown significantly, but there was no denying she was still far from the point she wanted to reach.

"I guess all I can do is keep trying to improve my accuracy... Huh?"

As she wiped her body down with a towel, an air-window opened up before her to announce a visitor.

No sooner did she recognize the gigantic young man projected in the display than the doors slid open.

"Well! It's been a while, Lester."

"...Hmph!" Seidoukan Academy's ninth-ranked fighter, Lester MacPhail, alias Kornephoros, snorted curtly as he straightened himself to his full height, staring down at Julis in challenge.

Lester and Julis had had their fair share of quarrels in the past, but since the Phoenix the previous year, they hadn't found themselves able to flare up at each other like they once had. And since this year Julis had been so busy training for the Gryps, this was her first time seeing him face-to-face in several months.

"...What on earth happened to you?" Julis asked with a frown.

Lester's body was nearly covered head to foot in bandages, and the areas that weren't looked heavily bruised.

Lester made a face. "Forget about it. It's no big deal."

"Hmm... If you say so. Then what brings you here?" she asked, although if she was being honest, she didn't particularly care.

"Isn't it obvious? Fight me, Julis."

"Huh...? This again? And I thought you'd grown up a little." Julis stared up at him with incredulity. "I don't think so. Stand aside please."

"...Why not?" The old Lester might have been incensed by her response, but this time, his voice was calm.

"Because I don't stand to gain anything from fighting you." Julis, beginning to wonder whether he might have matured a little, didn't mince her words.

"You can think of it as training! I heard you're entering the Lindvolus, right? So a fight with another Page One will be a valuable experience for you!"

"We've already done this three times over. Do you really think there's anything left for me to learn? No matter how you try to spin it, your fighting style is too set in stone. You might have made the Named Cult, but at this rate, even that will be in jeopardy sooner or later."

Perhaps Julis's chosen words were too strong, but Lester merely wrinkled his eyebrows in response. "You're right, of course… At least, you would have been, even just one month ago."

"Oh, so you're saying things have changed? And it only took a month?"

"See for yourself."

Throughout their exchange, Lester was managing to remain perfectly calm.

Mentally, at least, he did seem to have changed considerably.

"What if we made it a mock battle, with no effect on the rankings?"

"Hmm… Fine. If you really insist on it," Julis relented, activating her Rect Lux.

"Ha-ha! Now you're talking!" Lester exclaimed, immediately activating his own ax-shaped Lux, the Bardiche-Leo, and rushing toward her.

Julis's enthusiasm certainly didn't match his, but she did want to find out what was driving his sudden confidence now.

While she hadn't risen in rank, she was much stronger now than she had been two years ago. But Lester wasn't an idiot—he should have realized that.

And yet, *something* had emboldened him to challenge her.

As the automated voice announced the beginning of the mock battle, Julis concentrated her prana and waited for her opponent to make the first move.

Lester's fighting style essentially prioritized strength over technique and involved rapidly bringing himself down on his opponents in close combat to overwhelm them with his sheer power. Of course, he would take advantage of his opponent's weaknesses when they revealed themselves, like when he had fought Irene during the Phoenix, but Julis would provide no such obvious openings.

Indeed, while Julis had assumed from his bearing that he would begin with his usual swift assault, he instead braced himself, edging toward her carefully.

"Hmm… In that case, I'll go first! Burst into bloom—*Livingston Daisy!*"

Eight rings of flame materialized around her, before swooping down on her opponent.

"Arghhhhhhhhhh!"

Lester, as if he had read her intentions, charged forward with a terrific roar, mowing through the rings of flame before they could properly deploy.

And then—

"Meteor Arts…?!"

Smoke engulfed the room as Lester's battle-ax, having increased to a gargantuan size through mana excitation overload, extinguished the rings in a single stroke.

He immediately took advantage of that opening to close the distance between them.

His giant body emerged from the smoke, his battle-ax swinging down toward her—

"Nngh…!"

Julis managed to protect herself with her Rect Lux, but the impact was enough to send two of her four terminals flying through the air. Lester had always been among Seidoukan's best when it came to brute strength, and he seemed to have improved on it markedly since their last encounter.

Even so, the wide arc of his attack left a considerable opening.

Julis spun around his right-hand side, positioning her blade to strike directly at the school crest at his chest, when—

"I don't think so!" Lester cried out before it could reach its target, blocking her with his left arm and sending her crashing backward.

*Martial arts…?!*

The Meteor Arts that he had used a moment ago had been remark-

ably polished. Lester, it seemed, had finally found way to put his overabundance of prana to use.

On top of that, he was somehow wielding his humongous ax with one hand, forcing Julis backward in retreat.

At that moment, two of Julis's Rect Lux terminals swung around behind him, making their way toward him from his blind spot, but Lester, having already realized they were coming, brushed them both off before pulling back.

This, too, took Julis by surprise. Lester wasn't normally the kind of person to relent once he entered close combat, unless he had taken considerable damage.

"...I see. I guess I'll have to admit you weren't bluffing. How'd you do it in such short time?"

Their brief exchange was enough for Julis to notice the changes. He hadn't become dramatically stronger or anything like that. He was more powerful, true, but his speed and close-combat techniques weren't significantly different from how she remembered them.

There was one area, however, where he *had* most definitely improved.

His fighting style.

Where before he had been headstrong to the point of foolhardiness, now he was successfully managing to capitalize on his strongest asset, his raw power, to control the flow of the match. He had undergone rapid growth, but it was clearly based on how he had fought before—an ideal evolution of his distinct battle style, so to speak.

"Hmph! I'll let you know if you can beat me!" he declared with a dauntless laugh.

"Oh, will you now...? I'll hold you to that!"

Julis deployed her Rect Lux once more, using her rapier to carve a magic circle through the air.

"Burst into bloom—*Antirrhinum Majus!*"

He might have been able to dispel one of her more delicate techniques, but what about something on a larger scale?

The flames erupting around her took the form of a huge dragon, its wings spreading wide to either side as it swooped down toward him.

"Hah, I thought you'd try that one!"

Once more, Lester used Meteor Arts to make his battle-ax swell to an enormous size, before lashing out at the dragon head-on.

Though he swung his weapon downward with all his strength, sending the dragon crashing to the ground in an immediate explosion of flames, there was no chance he could have avoided the conflagration at that distance.

Nonetheless, he had, it seemed, shielded himself with his ax, swollen to enormous proportions thanks to his Meteor Arts.

"...Impressive, Lester!"

But he wasn't like Ayato or Orphelia—if he kept using Meteor Arts at the rate he was, he would soon exhaust his prana.

"I'll just have to finish this before that!" Lester, as if having read her mind, cried out as he charged toward her once more.

But Julis, having expected as much, had already set a trap directly in front of him.

"Blossom—*Gloriosa!*"

"Too easy!"

To escape the explosion erupting at his feet, Lester immediately leaped sideways—but the only way he could have done that was if he had known beforehand that she had set it there.

"...What?!" Julis cried in dismay.

"I thought you'd try that one!" Lester called out. He paused for a moment to catch his breath, before raising his ax overhead.

"I'm impressed... But it looks like *I'm* still better at reading *you*," Julis answered coolly as her second trap activated.

"Wha—?!"

"Blossom—*Semiserrata!*"

A camellia-like ball of flame unfolded above, engulfing Lester and Julis alike.

"Gaaaaah!"

Julis knew how to resist the explosion, but Lester had no such defense.

He tried to escape the rolling flames, but not before the tip of Julis's blade reached its target with a sharp clink.

"Looks like it's over."

"...Tch. So it didn't work after all," Lester grumbled as he raised his hand to his crest to admit defeat.

*"End of practice battle! Winner: Julis-Alexia von Riessfeld!"*

As the mechanical voice made its announcement, Lester, sprawled on the ground, breathed a heavy sigh. "I thought I'd last a bit longer at least..."

"No, to be honest, you almost had me. I'd have been in real danger if you had gotten close."

"Hmph. You still had other options open to you."

"...That's true."

Lester certainly had considerable power, but there was no denying the big difference in the speed and rate of his attacks compared with those of Ayato or Kirin. It would be hard to imagine him successfully getting the better of Julis as she was now.

At his current level of skill, that was.

But if what he had said earlier was true, and he really had improved so much over merely one month, then, assuming he kept working to maximize his potential, he might manage to reach a stage where Julis would be unable to best him.

"I'm sorry for looking down on you, Lester. Really," Julis said as she held out her hand.

Lester stared up at her with an expression she hadn't seen before. "You've changed, Julis."

"I don't need you to tell me that."

"Hmph, I guess not."

*He's certainly more self-conscious than he was before, too.*

"Well then..."

"Hold on—"

"I know," Lester said, rising to his feet and brushing the dust from his body. "A promise is a promise. I'll tell you what I've been doing this past month."

*

Ayato's home was located on the outskirts of a city in Japan's Shinshu region, around an hour by high-speed train from the North Kanto Mass-Impact Crater Lake.

After a short bus trip from the station, they found themselves standing in front of the gate leading to an imposing single-story Japanese-style house.

"Th-th-this is your h-h-house, Ayato?!" Kirin's voice wavered with tension.

"Yeah… Try to calm down a little, Kirin," Ayato said, flashing her a forced smile.

It was his first time home in a while as well, however, and he could barely keep his emotions from welling up inside him.

It was an old-fashioned building, connected to an adjoining dojo. It was surrounded by a garden that, while not particularly large, was meticulously maintained, and filled with memories of times he had shared with Haruka and Saya.

"U-um, maybe I *should* go get a present or something…" Kirin began turning back the way they had come.

"I told you, you don't need to worry about that," Ayato replied, grabbing her by the collar.

"B-but your father might think it rude of me, and I—I…" Kirin's voice trailed off. She looked as if she were about to break down in tears.

"He doesn't care about things like that. Or rather, he doesn't like people fussing over him, so you'd probably be fine even if you *were* a bit rude. So feel free to take what you want from the fridge, for example…"

"I—I couldn't do that!"

*No, I guess not…*

That would be asking too much of her.

"Anyway, let's go."

"O-okay...!"

Ayato opened the door to the entryway and invited Kirin in, but the house was silent. There was no sign of any occupants.

"Um..."

"Ah, he's probably in the dojo," Ayato realized, urging the bewildered Kirin to follow him.

From what Ayato understood, the head dojo of the Amagiri Shinmei style wasn't presently taking any students.

After Ayato's victory at the Phoenix, Claudia had told him she would have Galaxy make sure things didn't get hectic at his home, and they certainly seemed to have accomplished that.

So what could his father, the head of the Amagiri Shinmei style, be doing in the dojo?

The answer was obvious.

"...Dad? I'm home," Ayato called out quietly to the man silently meditating in the darkness—his father, Masatsugu.

"So you're back."

Ayato couldn't help but be astonished at the sight of his father as the man slowly opened his eyes and, without a further word, smoothly rose to his feet. His movements, as usual, were perfectly guarded.

His status as the head of the Amagiri Shinmei style was no empty title.

He had a strongly trained physique that belied his years; a solemn, severe countenance; and above all, a stern presence. He hadn't changed at all from how Ayato remembered him.

"U-um, h-h-how do you do! I'm Kirin Toudou!" Kirin blurted out, bowing down ninety degrees.

At this, Masatsugu shifted his attention to her for the first time. "Ah... The girl from the Toudou style. I should thank you for taking care of my son. I don't have much to offer, but please, make yourself at home."

"Th-thank you...! But, uh...?" Kirin turned toward Ayato, as if only now realizing something. "Um, your father isn't...?" she murmured doubtfully.

"Ah, right...," Ayato responded, his voice equally low. "I guess I forgot to mention it. But no, my dad isn't a Genestella."

At this, Kirin's gaze flickered back and forth between them in astonishment.

# CHAPTER 3
# FATHER AND MOTHER

"…"

Ayato and Masatsugu moved their chopsticks in utter silence. Masatsugu was an uncommunicative person in general, opening his mouth only when something needed to be done. It was, of course, difficult to talk to someone with that kind of personality, so Ayato had long since given up trying to engage him in conversation.

Indeed, dinner tonight at the Amagiri household was just as it always was.

Things had been different when Haruka had been there. She had acted as a sort of intermediary between the two of them, effortlessly helping the conversation flow around her.

Dinner was simmered fish with sautéed lotus root, boiled *komatsuna*, and miso soup with fried tofu and radish. Ayato and Masatsugu had cooked everything themselves.

It certainly tasted like home cooking, but Ayato couldn't help but feel that the flavors were somehow different whenever he or his father were responsible for them. His image of home cooking was Haruka's cooking, or else the kind of thing that Saya's mother, Kaya, would put together.

"Kirin, please don't hold back."

"Y-yes… Thank you…," she said with a relieved nod.

Ayato was used to this atmosphere, but she probably found it stifling.

"Well, I guess it isn't anything special, though."

"No, it's very nice!" But despite her words, there was something unnatural about the movement of her chopsticks.

She was probably still nervous.

"B-by the way... What were you like as a child, Ayato?" she asked, probably trying to lighten the mood.

"I was just a normal kid, I suppose," Ayato answered with a smile.

At this, Masatsugu, his countenance unchanging, spoke up: "He was the kind of kid who didn't follow instructions."

"Come on, Dad..." But seeing Kirin give a real, unfeigned smile for the first time since they had arrived, Ayato couldn't bring himself to say anything stronger.

"Ha-ha, so you *were* a troublemaker!"

"He'd quarrel with the students. He'd get serious when it came to training, but he always strayed too far from the set forms."

"So *now* you open your mouth...," Ayato muttered as he stared into his food.

Kirin, watching on from the side, shook with laughter.

"Kirin?" Ayato wondered.

"Ah, s-sorry... It's just, this is the first time I've seen you like this."

"Like this?"

"How do I put it... Acting your age?" she answered, tilting her head slightly to one side.

"Huh? R-really?"

He was slightly taken aback by her words, perhaps because he hadn't realized it for himself.

"Does he normally act more mature?" Masatsugu's question only added to Ayato's surprise.

"Um...," Kirin answered, pondering. "Rather than mature... calmer, maybe, or more easygoing?"

"Oh? That *does* come as a surprise."

Ayato hadn't realized *that* either—nor, by the looks of it, had his father.

There was no denying, however, that Kirin had succeeded in brightening the mood somewhat.

Ayato was finally able to relax during the family meal in a way he hadn't been able to in a long time.

And then—

"Ah, let me do the washing up," Kirin said when they were finished, as she began gathering the tableware.

"You don't need to worry about that, Kirin. We'd never make a guest—"

"Thank you, Miss Toudou. That would be a great help."

"Dad...?" Ayato glanced toward him, only for his father to stare back at him with a meaningful gaze.

Ayato—and, it seemed, Kirin too—could guess what he meant.

In short, he was asking her to leave the room.

As Kirin left for the kitchen, the dishes and cutlery gathered on a tray, Masatsugu straightened his posture, his expression growing even sterner.

Right. Masatsugu had invited Ayato home because he had something he wanted to tell him.

"...What is it?"

"It's about Haruka." Masatsugu headed, as ever, straight to the point—not that Ayato hadn't expected as much.

"Oh...? So now you want to talk about her," Ayato said in a low voice, his eyes narrowed.

His father hadn't appeared to be particularly worried when Haruka had first disappeared.

Not only would he brush aside any suggestion that they go and look for her when Ayato so much as mentioned her disappearance but Masatsugu would also simply tell him that they should respect her wishes.

That was ultimately why their relationship had deteriorated so dramatically.

"You haven't even come to see her. Not even once."

It was close to a year now since Ayato had found her, after all.

All his father had to do was go to the hospital in Asterisk. There should have been nothing stopping him from doing that.

"...I'll go when she wakes up."

"That isn't the problem!" Ayato blurted out, before forcing his eyes shut.

Things always ended up like this when the two of them spoke about Haruka.

"...Sorry."

It was a little late, but what Kirin had said earlier came back to him. He *did* have a habit of acting childish in front of his father.

He tried to calm the waves beating at his heart—but the self-possession that he had finally managed to restore was soon brought crashing down with only a few short words.

"Listen, Ayato... Haruka isn't my daughter."

"...What?"

Ayato had difficulty comprehending what his father was trying to say.

"At first, I thought it would be better for you to hear it from Haruka herself, but now...now that it's come to this, I guess we've got no choice. You're older now than she was back then. You should be able to deal with it."

"H-hold on a minute, Dad... What are you saying...?"

Ayato, unable to believe those words that had already begun to seep deep into his heart, shook his head weakly.

"When I first met your mother...when I first met Sakura, she was already pregnant—with Haruka."

Sakura Amagiri was Ayato's mother.

"But that would mean..." It would mean that they were really half-siblings, with different fathers. "Th-that can't be! I mean, in that case, Haruka's real father—"

"I never asked your mother. I never looked into her life before she entered mine, or had anyone else look into it. And she never told me about it. Only..." Masatsugu paused there for a moment, though when he continued, his voice was as matter-of-fact as ever. "I don't know exactly when or how she found out, but your sister seems to have realized that I'm not her real father."

"Wha—?!"

Ayato was lost for words.

The Haruka he remembered had always been gentle and composed. Not once did he remember her ever seeming worried or depressed.

But no, there were exceptions to that—like the day she had placed his seal on him.

"No! So you're saying that her disappearance had something to do with that?!"

"Maybe."

But if that was true, why had she gone so far as to put that seal on him? *"I'll protect you. That's why."* That was what she had said back then. But what did she mean by that? And why had she thrown herself into something as dangerous as the Eclipse?

Ayato didn't understand any of it.

*I guess the only to find way to find out is to ask her directly...*

He let out a resigned sigh, before glancing back up at his father. "Dad, I've got something I need to discuss with you as well."

"...What?"

"It's about waking her. They might be able to do it as my wish for winning the Gryps, but I'm not—"

"Do whatever you think is best," Masatsugu interrupted before he could finish.

"...Huh?"

Ayato couldn't hold back the feelings of resentment that surged forth at his father's apparent lack of concern.

"What's that supposed to mean?! You could at least hear me out!"

"There's no need."

"You're always like this! You don't listen to anything I have to say!"

Ayato stared down at the table, grinding his teeth.

*Why did it have to come to this?*

No, he should have known that it would. His father held himself to a strict, unwavering rule—one that Ayato didn't fully comprehend.

Haruka had understood him, but not Ayato.

"…Just let me ask you one more thing."

If his father was going to be so recalcitrant, he would ask him something that he *should* be able to answer.

Ayato forced himself to bury his anger and stifle his emotions before continuing. "What was Mom like? What kind of person was she?"

If Haruka had left home to search for her real father, Ayato's sole connection to that endeavor was his mother, Sakura.

Ayato had no strong memories of her. He remembered pestering Masatsugu and Haruka to tell him about her when he had been young, but there had been no sense of tangible reality to the person they had described.

Masatsugu remained silent for a moment, deep in thought, before responding. "She was…strong."

That wasn't the answer Ayato had been hoping for, but he could sense real emotion in his father's words.

It was enough to give him the peace of mind that he needed, at least in part.

"I see. Thank you."

But with that, there was nothing left for the two of them to discuss. Ayato rose to his feet, quietly making his way from the room.

\*

*"So Haruka Amagiri is* your *daughter,"* Dirk Eberwein said from the other side of the air-window, his voice and expression as sour as ever.

"Oh…? That's some excellent probing you've done there." Madiath, impressed, smiled back at him, putting his hands together in exaggerated applause. "You wouldn't guess how long it took *me* to find her."

Madiath's office was illuminated only by the faint light of the moon outside and the air-window in front of him. The shadows were where he preferred to reside.

*"Hmph. It wasn't that hard, with all these clues lying around."*

"Hmm. I suppose not."

No, it was only a matter of time before anyone looking into Ayato Amagiri also looked into his mother. The problem was what came after that, but if you took Dirk's special talents into account—or rather, the special talents of those who served as his eyes and ears—it was by no means impossible to pull back the curtain.

*"Who would have guessed that Akari Yachigusa could still be alive?"*

"…She isn't."

How many years had it been, Madiath wondered, since he had heard that name said aloud?

Akari Yachigusa—his one and only tag partner, someone who now only existed deep in his buried past.

*"Ah, is that so? The records all say she passed away quite a while back. The year after you two won the Phoenix, in fact."*

"Exactly."

*"The thing is—she actually changed her face, her name, even her past, and started a new life. But there's no way that a Strega like Akari Yachigusa could turn into someone else so suddenly. Not that easily. There's no way the IEFs would stand for it. Which means—"*

"Very perceptive of you. Yes, that was her wish after winning the Festa. And who else could grant it but them? Although, I only realized it myself after she had already left our fair city," Madiath said jokingly, with a shrug of his shoulders. "And what exactly are you trying to accomplish, digging up the past like this?"

*"I couldn't care less about this…gossip. I just don't want you to let your personal feelings get in the way of what we're doing,"* Dirk said, his gaze growing sharper.

"Heh, it's a bit late for that… You and me, we're both driven by personal feelings, if you look back far enough. Aren't we?"

*"Quit screwing around. You've kept Haruka Amagiri alive this long, and you've been watching from the sidelines while Ayato Amagiri takes the crown at the Gryps. It's all connected."*

Yes, it was truly impressive how Dirk had managed to connect the dots.

At this point, Madiath wouldn't have been surprised if his counterpart already knew about that night, too.

But be that as it may—

"Now, now, there's no need for this suspicion of yours. If I killed her, I'd never be able to undo the seal placed on me. That's the only reason she's still alive."

*"If that's all you're after, you could get that lunatic woman to do it for you. From what I hear, she's been saying as much to nearly anyone who'll listen."*

"And would you be willing to part with Miss Orphelia in compensation?"

It certainly wouldn't be impossible for Hilda to dispel the ability, but she could be guaranteed to want to take advantage of the situation. It didn't require much thought to work out what she would demand.

"I'm sure she's fully aware of our state of affairs. She won't be likely to compromise. So speaking for myself, I'm not willing to give up our ace just yet."

*"You shameless little...! Firstly, it all depends on Ayato Amagiri, and he wants to wake her up right away! So what are you gonna do?"*

"There's no need to worry about that. I've taken precautions." Madiath leaned back into his chair with a composed smile. "Ayato Amagiri won spectacularly, as expected. Thanks to him, we now have our first chance in decades for a Festa that could end in a grand slam. The excitement is palpable, and most advantageous as far as the plan is concerned, wouldn't you say?"

*"I'll give you that. And the council has almost reached a decision. Still..."* Dirk paused there, his eyes gleaming with something bordering on hatred. *"You'd better not have forgotten. It was Haruka Amagiri who wrecked our plans last time."*

"I understand that. Much better than you do. It was me, Varda, and Ecknardt who put those plans together in the first place. You were simply riding on our coattails."

The plan six years ago had fallen apart at the final stage, at Haruka's hand, exactly as Dirk had said.

The Golden Bough Alliance had lost an irreplaceable member, forcing Madiath and the others to start over from square one.

"I am, of course, grateful for your assistance. But I don't think you have the right to talk about the previous plan like that."

"...*Tch!*" Dirk clicked his tongue in anger, and with that, the air-window snapped shut.

"Good grief... Just how many times are we going to have this kind of conversation?" Madiath murmured as he rubbed his shoulders, when Varda appeared out of the darkness in the corner of the room.

"Who is this Akari Yachigusa?"

"Oh, so you're interested in a human, for once?"

"That's my line. There are very few humans to whom you're so attached. I'm aware of Haruka and Ayato Amagiri, but this is the first I've heard of this one." The urm-manadite core at Varda's chest began to glow ominously.

"That's only natural, considering she's from before I met you. But if you're asking who she was... Hmm. That's a tough one. She was stupidly naive. The kind of person who loved loneliness and solitude but couldn't stand being left alone. Who adored children and cherry blossoms. And..." Madiath rested his chin in his hand as he sank deep into thought, staring into the night sky outside his window. "Yes, if I had to sum her up in one word—she was weak."

\*

Kirin, having finished washing the dishes and tidying up, was making her way back to the living room when she bumped into Ayato in the corridor.

"Ah, Ayato—"

"...Sorry, Kirin. I'm stepping out for a bit," he interrupted, his gaze downcast, before quickening his pace and making for the entrance.

"Ah..." Kirin could do nothing more than watch as he disappeared into the night. Head tilted slightly to one side, she slid open the Japanese-style door to the living room, glancing toward Masatsugu. "Um, Ayato just—"

"Don't worry about him," the older man said softly, glancing briefly in her direction. "He'll come back."

"I—I see..."

It was clear that *something* must have happened between the two of them, but there was nothing she could do about it. For a second, she had thought about chasing after him, but when she stopped to put her thoughts in order, she realized that she didn't even know where he had gone, so that was impossible.

She had no choice but to drop her gaze and take a nearby seat.

"..."

Kirin lost track of time in that awkward silence, until finally—

"I'm afraid I'm not very good with words," Masatsugu began.

His expression was still as intense as it had been a moment ago, but to Kirin, he looked terribly disheartened.

"Their mother always said she wanted them both to be free. To have the freedom she didn't. But even with freedom, people still have to take responsibility for themselves. So I was strict with them. I tried to bring them both up so they would understand that... Haruka did. She was always mature for her age." Masatsugu opened up in his usual matter-of-fact tone of voice.

Though Kirin sat nearby, he seemed to be talking more to himself than to her.

"Even when he left to go to Asterisk, Ayato still didn't seem ready to me. But then...seeing him today for the first time in a year and a half, well... He's grown up. I probably have you to thank for that, and your friends." With that, Masatsugu bowed deeply before her.

"Huh? N-n-not at all...!" Kirin stammered, waving her hands.

"If he's still lost, still looking for something, it's probably because he's carrying a burden inside himself. But that isn't my place to interfere."

He would be better off having this discussion with Ayato directly, Kirin thought.

But he was probably only able to speak so freely with her precisely *because* she was an outsider.

Because they were so close, certain invisible walls tended to pop up between family members. She understood that only too well.

After he had finished confiding in her, Masatsugu took a deep breath, before rising to his feet. "Well then—I'm sorry to bore you with our troubles, Miss Toudou. I don't mean this as an excuse, but he's in your hands now."

"M-me...?" Kirin echoed, unsure what he meant.

"He's wavering, like he doesn't know how best to strike with his blade," Masatsugu continued slowly. "I might not be worth much as a parent, but I do know the way of the sword. In that respect, at least, I can offer you both advice."

"Oh..."

That *was* why she had come to the Amagiri household in the first place. It wasn't as if it had slipped her mind, but she hadn't wanted it to get in the way of their father-son discussion.

"P-please...!" She stood up in a hurry, quickly bowing her head.

"Then come to the dojo," Masatsugu replied with a firm nod.

After the two of them changed into their martial arts uniforms, they proceeded barefoot onto the impeccably polished floorboards of the dojo.

"Let's start by looking at your form. Yes... Try to come at me from above."

"B-but...," Kirin stammered.

Masatsugu wasn't a Genestella. While they might only be using wooden practice blades, it would be inexcusable for her to try to hit him with her full strength.

And yet—

"Wow!"

The moment Masatsugu adopted his fighting posture, Kirin felt a rush of admiration at how perfect it was. She couldn't help but feel as if she were looking at a thing of beauty.

At the very least, there could be no doubt that Masatsugu was a master.

That being the case, it would be rude of her to be more cautious than absolutely necessary, Kirin thought to steady herself, before raising her blade over her head.

She calmed her breathing—and stepped forward to strike her opponent.

"—!"

The blow, aimed, she had thought, directly at Masatsugu's head, fell short by a fraction of an inch.

No. Strictly speaking, he had brushed it aside.

Masatsugu had made a half-step forward as she lunged toward him, using both his momentum and hers to ward off her attack with his own blade.

"I see... Just as I've heard, the Toudou style truly is a work of genius." Masatsugu nodded in praise.

Kirin stared back in astonishment. "How did you...?"

"Surprised? Even us ordinary folk can do this much with proper discipline and training," Masatsugu declared. "Of course, as far as raw strength is concerned, I'm quite sure I'll be no match for you. Both Haruka and Ayato surpassed me in that respect long ago. No, us ordinary folk fall far short of you Genestella in both speed and strength. Let's say I were to face off against you in earnest. At most, I'd probably only be able to hold my own for a few seconds."

"...Yes."

He was probably right about that. Even if an ordinary person managed to block her attack, she would likely be able to overwhelm them through strength alone. On top of that, it would be close to impossible for them to properly judge her movements, and even if they did, they wouldn't be able to move fast enough to counter them.

Genestella were simply more capable in that respect.

So what, she wondered, had just happened?

"But if your movements are limited, like they were only a moment ago, I'll still have some options available. And luckily for me, the state of mind fostered by the Amagiri Shinmei style's *shiki* technique also helps."

"Options...?"

"Techniques," Masatsugu corrected himself. "Someone like me certainly can't surpass a Genestella in physical ability, but I can train myself in techniques. The key lies in precision, in how thoroughly you can put yourself into one swing of the sword. You've yet to master that, which is why someone like me was able to block your attack."

Certainly, there could be no question that technique was more important than strength, and the same went for speed. Even if it was harder to evade an attack with great destructive power, that didn't change the basic principle.

"Now, I'll try to do the same."

"…Yes!"

Kirin raised her practice blade in front of her.

Masatsugu, on the other hand, held his at his side, before lunging forwards and sweeping it toward her chest, quickly twisting his wrist to slash downward.

It was the Amagiri Shinmei style's Twin Serpents technique—a move Ayato himself used often.

There was something different about it, though. When Ayato used it, his movements were certainly both faster and stronger, and yet Masatsugu's technique was far more formidable.

The attack was sharp—so sharp, it seemed, that if she were to make one wrong move it might cut clean through her practice blade.

The second she understood that, Kirin felt a wave of inspiration and shame rush through her.

How shallow had she been, how foolish, how conceited, to think that she, still so inexperienced, didn't know where next to take her own swordsmanship?

"Um, can you show me more?" Kirin asked, her eyes sparkling as she readied herself for a third time.

"Of course." Masatsugu gave her a strong nod, the corners of his lips curling up ever so slightly in a faint but unmistakably warm smile.

# CHAPTER 4
# HARUKA AMAGIRI

Ayato was walking along the narrow path that ran deep through the forest.

As he edged his way forward with the help of the wan moonlight, he felt not forlorn but, rather, almost as he had as a child, when he had traversed this path almost daily. He knew these woods like the back of his hand. He had no difficulty winding his way toward his destination.

"…This brings back memories."

A small clearing suddenly opened up in the depths of the forest. This had been where he had spent the majority of his free time back when he was kid.

It had been a long time since he had last come here, and now that he saw it again, it looked somehow narrower than he remembered it.

He glanced up to the moon glowing high in the winter sky, before sitting down on a bower at the edge of the clearing and closing his eyes in an attempt to put his thoughts in order.

If what his father had said was true—and there was no reason why it wouldn't be—then he and Haruka were actually half-siblings.

But that wasn't the issue right now. Even if they were only half-related by blood, she was still, after all, his sister. His feelings there hadn't changed.

It was just—

"If her disappearance had something to do with her real father, though…"

That seemed likely—or rather, no other possibilities came to mind.

In a way, it was almost inevitable that things would have come to this. It was only natural that someone would want to know about their true heritage. But that wasn't the kind of thing that he could just butt in on—it was something Haruka herself had to deal with.

And yet—

"What if her real father has some kind of connection to me, too…?"

But no, that couldn't be right.

Ayato didn't know Haruka's reason for putting his seal on him, but there was no way it was unrelated to her disappearance.

There was one thing they had in common, one thing that transcended everything else…

"Mom."

But Ayato wasn't able to follow that train of thought any further.

He couldn't help but wonder whether what his father had said was true, whether his mother truly hadn't ever spoken about her past. But Masatsugu wasn't shrewd enough to tell such a barefaced lie.

"Mom's past…," he murmured under his breath as he tried to call her face to mind.

He could remember her only faintly. He didn't even have any photographs or videos of her.

"I need to ask Haruka directly… But to do that, I'd have to—"

At that moment, his mobile began to ring.

He opened an air-window, and a somewhat drained voice rang out. *"Yoo-hoo!"*

"…Saya? Is everything okay?"

On the other side of the air-window, his childhood friend waved back at him. *"You said you were going home today, so I thought it'd probably take you until around now to calm down."* She paused there, frowning in suspicion. *"Is something wrong?"*

"…You're too perceptive, Saya."

He hadn't intended to let his feelings show. He couldn't help but feel a touch of shame that she had been able to see through him so easily.

"*Did you have a fight with your dad?*" Saya asked worriedly. "*Is it that bad between you two?*"

Saya knew, of course, that Ayato's relationship with his father was strained, but she no doubt remembered Masatsugu as he had been during their childhood. Their relationship might not have been good, exactly, back when Haruka had still been with them, but at least it had by no means been bad.

"It's fine. It's no big deal, really," Ayato replied, trying to set her at ease.

"*...You're a bad liar.*" Saya, however, saw right through him. "*But if you don't want to talk about it, I won't ask.*"

"Thanks..."

This was a problem he had to solve by himself. If he ended up relying on someone else, it would be only more difficult to find an answer.

"*By the way... Are you in that clearing in the forest?*"

"Ah, yeah. You know me too well, I guess."

The air-window was, of course, projecting his image to Saya, too, but his surroundings were almost pitch black, and while the air window itself emitted a faint light, it was only strong enough to outline his face.

"*I do remember it, you know? It's where we both went to play, after all.*"

"Ha-ha, right. We did come here a lot, didn't we?"

Now that he thought about it, it was here where he and Saya had challenged Haruka.

"*Ayato, do you remember? That's where we had our first match over those wish coupons.*"

"Of course I remember. I lost. I was pretty upset, actually."

They had repeated those matches practically every day—sometimes even multiple times each day.

"*Which reminds me, your first wish... Ah, right. Your mom found out that you wet the bed, and you wanted us to go and apologize together—*"

*"You should forget about that one."* Saya averted her gaze, her cheeks turning red in embarrassment. *"But if you want to bring that up, don't forget the time you…"*

The two of them remained that way for a long while: exchanging fond stories of their childhood together. Ayato soon found his mood lightening.

"Thanks, Saya."

*"Don't mention it."*

While he had ended up leaving most of the talking to her, Saya simply smiled back at him warmly.

"I had better get going—"

"A-Ayato!" came a trembling voice from amid the darkness, seemingly on the verge of breaking down into tears.

When he turned around, he could see Kirin fumbling through the trees, flashlight in hand, cautiously making her way toward him one step at a time.

"Huh…? Kirin?" Ayato called back.

At the sound of his voice, her expression suddenly lit up, and she rushed forward. "I—I didn't know what to do… Y-you didn't come back, and—"

"Sorry for making you worry. But how did you know I was here?"

"That's… Your father said to look here…"

"Dad did?" Ayato was slightly taken aback by the unexpected answer.

Just how long had Masatsugu known about this place?

But that surprise was soon drowned out by a cold, emotionless voice coming from behind him. *"Ayato."* He could feel Saya glaring at him. *"What's Kirin doing there…?"*

"Huh? Ah, n-no, I mean, that's…"

Ayato glanced toward Kirin, trying to come up with some kind of explanation, but her face had turned scarlet, and she stood waving her hands in panic.

"Ah, um, Saya, this isn't—"

*"Got it. I'm coming over. Now. Right now. I don't care what it takes. I'm definitely coming."*

"B-b-but Saya! I mean, you need permission!"

Whenever students wanted to leave Asterisk, they had to apply to do so in advance. While it wasn't particularly difficult to get permission over the vacation periods, applications weren't processed immediately, let alone in the middle of the night. On top of that, the ferryboat service had already finished.

*"I'll swim if I have to. It's okay, I've prepared some underwater Luxes for times like this. He-he-he..."*

Saya looked to be getting quite worked up, her eyes darting to and fro. Ayato had known her for a long time, but he had never seen this side of her before.

It took him and Kirin upwards of thirty minutes to convince her that everything was okay.

"Phew... It's gotten pretty late," Ayato said as they made their way back to the house.

"Y-yes..." Kirin, walking along beside him, nodded.

"I'm really sorry about running off like that, especially after inviting you to come visit..."

"N-not at all! Thanks to you, I've been able to find my way!"

"Huh?" Ayato, surprised, glanced up at her—and sure enough, Kirin did look somewhat refreshed.

"Your father gave me some advice and training."

"Ah..."

That was enough for him to realize what she meant.

As a swordsman, Masatsugu was worthy of unreserved respect. There could be no questioning his skill or ability to teach.

"I can't say that I really know where I'm going yet, but...at least I'll be able to face my great-aunt now."

"I see... That's good to hear," Ayato replied with a smile, when Kirin came to a sudden halt.

"U-um...!"

"Yeah?"

"I don't mean to be rude, but why don't you... Why don't you train with him a little too?" Kirin gripped his hands tightly, gazing up at him earnestly. "Your father really is a wonderful swordsman. So I thought, maybe if you two trained together, you'd be able to better understand each other's thoughts!"

That was a remarkably forward proposal coming from her, Ayato thought. It must have taken her considerable courage to voice that suggestion. Her concern for him was nothing if not heartwarming.

Nonetheless, he shook his head. "He sure is a good swordsman…"

But it wasn't that side of Masatsugu who he wanted to speak with—what he needed right now was his father. And so long as Masatsugu had a sword in hand, there was no way that that part of him would come forth. That was the kind of person he was, for better or for worse.

"Ah…" Perhaps having read his expression, Kirin hung her head in dejection.

"Anyway, I'm glad he helped you think things through," Ayato said, patting her on the head.

"…"

Kirin stared back at him, looking as if she had something that she wanted to say, but in the end, she remained silent.

*

Kirin awoke shortly before dawn the next morning, sitting up from her futon and rubbing her eyes.

The Amagiri household's guestroom was in a Japanese style, eight tatami mats in size. Apart from a hanging scroll in the recessed alcove, there were no decorations to speak of, but it was thoroughly cleaned from corner to corner, and the crisp winter air that had made its way inside left her feeling fresh and invigorated.

She was used to waking up early for her morning training. Wondering what she should do in her unfamiliar surroundings, she set about her daily routine, folding up the futon, getting dressed, and stepping outside to splash her face with the piercingly cold water, when, as she made her way back, she heard sounds coming from the kitchen.

She proceeded nervously down the corridor, the floorboards creaking beneath her, only to find Masatsugu preparing breakfast.

"Good morning. Did you sleep well?"

"Y-yes!" Kirin responded, bowing her head. "Good morning! Um, can I help?"

Masatsugu looked her over in silence for a moment, before nodding. "There should be an apron in the drawer over there."

Inside the indicated drawer was a cute, neatly-folded, pink apron. It was unlikely that either Masatsugu or Ayato used it, so it must have been Haruka's.

She wondered for a second whether it was really okay for her to use it, but she didn't have much choice now. She would just borrow it for a moment and then put it back.

"I'll slice some pickles, then."

Until Kirin had come to Asterisk, she had had no experience cooking, but since working with Saya to make lunch for Ayato, she had been able to find time to practice every now and then. She had been clumsy from the very beginning, and there was no mistaking that she still had a long way to go, but at least now she could handle a knife without cutting herself.

She removed the pickles from the salted rice bran as instructed by the senior Amagiri then washed away the residue and cut them into neat pieces.

"…Huh? Kirin?" Ayato, late to get out of bed, stood wide-eyed as he stared at them.

"Ah, good morning, Ayato!"

"Morning… Is that Haruka's apron?"

So she had been right…

"Ah, um, I guess I shouldn't have…?"

"No, it looks good on you. It's just…" Ayato stood staring at it strangely for a moment, somewhat wistfully. "Anyway, you're a guest, so you don't need to worry about all these chores."

"No, this is the least I can do to thank you for both for your hospitality."

"Hmm… Well, if that's what you want…"

Faced with her enthusiasm for the task, he said no more than that. Instead, he turned his gaze to Masatsugu.

"Dad, I'll be going back to Asterisk today."

"Huh?" Kirin, surprised, stayed her hand on the cutting board. "Y-you're going back already?"

"Yeah. It looks like coming here helped you out. And besides, you should probably head back to your place, too. Your father must be waiting for you."

That was no doubt true, but there should have been no need for *him* to leave after only one day, especially when he hadn't been home in so long.

Kirin glanced across the room to see Masatsugu, stoic as ever, give Ayato a curt nod. "Fine. Do as you wish."

*These two blockheads!*

She knew, as an outsider, that she shouldn't try to interfere too much, but she couldn't help but be frustrated by the both of them.

*Haruka must really have been amazing if she could get these two to get along...*

She let out a deep sigh, staring down at the pink apron.

Kirin had only ever seen Haruka's sleeping figure, when she had gone with the other members of Team Enfield to visit her in her hospital room, and didn't know what she was like as a person. Appearance-wise, she had gentle features, a lot like Ayato's. Saya claimed that she was even stronger than her younger brother, but that would mean—

"We're ready here," Masatsugu announced, having finished cooking the fish.

The pickles were ready, too.

"...Ayato?" Kirin asked.

"Ah." He handed her the plates.

"Th-thank you."

*They get along normally enough here, though...*

But that was probably because they hadn't said much.

Ayato, seemingly worried about her, said a few words to her during breakfast, but hardly even glanced his father's way.

To be honest, the atmosphere was even gloomier than it had been the night before.

"Well, Kirin, let me know when you're ready."

"Y-yes..."

Ayato said that he would do the washing up, so Kirin went back to her room.

She didn't have much to put away, having only been there for a night and two meals, but wanting to leave everything as clean as she had found it, she set about tidying everything up, when she heard a noise coming from the adjacent room.

Stepping out into the corridor, she found that the door leading into it was slightly ajar.

She didn't want whoever it was to think that she was spying on them, so she tried calling out softly. "Um...?"

"Ah, Kirin." It was Masatsugu.

"Is this...?"

"...It's Haruka's room." His tone of voice was as flat as ever, but Kirin couldn't help but wonder whether she hadn't detected a hint of sadness mixed into it.

"S-sorry for intruding...," she murmured, before timidly entering.

For a high school girl's room, it was surprisingly modest (though strictly speaking, her own room back at her own house was very similar, so she couldn't really comment on what a normal one might look like).

There was a desk, a bed, several small containers and boxes for storage, and a bookcase filled with countless old tomes—no doubt books on sword techniques.

Kirin could see right away that this room was as scrupulously maintained as the guestroom and the dojo. It had probably been this way ever since Haruka had left for Asterisk.

So that she could come home whenever she wanted.

*So I was right...*

Ayato and Masatsugu both felt the same way toward her.

They just weren't good at letting each other know that.

"Um… What kind of person was Ayato's sister?" Kirin asked.

Masatsugu glanced toward a small, manadite-powered photo frame by the side of the bed.

It switched on through sight alone, opening up several small air-windows.

"Wow…"

Taken aback by the rapid flood of images, Kirin glanced from the first one to the next, a feeling of warmth bubbling up inside her at the happy family photos.

The pictures showed Haruka, Ayato, Masatsugu, and even occasionally Saya and her family in the middle of normal, everyday activities.

In every single one of them, Ayato was smiling. He indeed looked slightly mischievous, as Masatsugu had said the night before, with an adorable grin.

Masatsugu's expression had been as severe as it was now, but the air around him seemed somehow softer.

At that moment, Kirin realized that Ayato hadn't shown her a genuine smile since they had arrived here.

*This isn't good…*

She didn't know exactly why, but she felt it in her heart.

They couldn't afford to leave things the way they were.

"U-um…"

But just before she could open her mouth, Masatsugu spoke up. "Kirin," he began softly. "I'll leave Ayato to you." And with that, he bowed deeply.

"Th-that's…! I mean, I'm the one who's always being saved by him!" She stepped backward, flustered.

"I watched the Gryps," Masatsugu continued. "If he had stayed here, Ayato wouldn't have grown as much as he has. I'm indebted to you and your friends."

Sensing the sincerity imbued in those words, Kirin could do nothing but remain silent.

"He can be reckless, sometimes. If you can, please, stand by him when he needs you."

"…Yes. I'll do my best," she answered.

Only then did Masatsugu raise his head.

"We'll be off, then." Ayato swung his bag over his shoulder and stepped outside.

His father had come to see them off, but he said nothing as he watched them go. Ayato said no more either.

"Thank you for everything." Kirin bowed her head in thanks, before chasing after her schoolmate.

The weather had undergone a sudden change, the sky dull and cloudy. The wind wasn't strong, but the cold was enough to tear into her skin.

"Right, the station is—"

"Um, Ayato…!" Kirin called out, having made up her mind.

Ayato, several paces in front of her, came to a stop, looking over his shoulder. "Hmm? What's wrong?"

"Um, I mean…"

He shone her his usual easygoing smile. Or at least, that was how it looked.

But she was right—there was something different about it. It wasn't *real*.

"Ayato, are you really going back to Rikka like this?"

As much as she wanted to, she couldn't tell him to go back and see his father. Even if the two of them did talk, they still probably wouldn't resolve their issues. And more importantly, she had no right to stick her nose into things.

"That's the plan…"

"In that case…"

What, she wondered, would Saya, his closest friend, say? Or Julis, whom Ayato had first set out to help? Or, for that matter, Claudia, who always had him on her mind?

She didn't know the answer to any of those questions.

But that was precisely why she knew what she had to do next.

"Th-then, why don't you… I mean, you could c-c-come to my place with me…," she stammered, grabbing onto the edge of his coat.

"Huh...?" Ayato's eyes widened in surprise.

"No, I mean, um..." She mustered her wavering voice, only too aware of the blood rising to her cheeks. "I mean, when you invited me, it was because you were coming home, and if you're finished here, then...um..."

Anyway, she wanted him to stay with her. Even if there was no real need or reason for him to do so, she wanted him to remain by her side.

"Hmm..." He stood motionless as he mulled over the sudden invitation.

"A-and since you invited me to your house, I—I want to return the favor... I mean, your father taught me a little of the Amagiri Shinmei style, so why don't you let me show you the Toudou style too...?"

Rikka—Asterisk— was, above all, a place of battle.

Kirin didn't dislike the city, but there were certain things you just couldn't find there, certain things you couldn't learn. Having left its borders, having ventured into the outside world, Kirin had come to understand that all the more acutely. There were things you could polish there, but also things you couldn't. And unless you are able to change yourself along the way, you could end up breaking.

She didn't know whether or not Ayato had realized that, but this time, it was her turn to help him.

"...All right," he replied after a long moment, flashing her a forced smile. "As long as it isn't any trouble. I *do* want to say hello to your dad, and I *am* interested in the Toudou style."

"O-of course! He'll be so pleased to see you!" Overjoyed, Kirin made a small fist, mentally leaping into the air in triumph.

*

Ladislav Bartošik was being detained in a mansion on a small island in the South Seas.

He had been apprehended on eleven charges as the ideological mastermind behind the Jade Twilight Incident, but as his trial had been completely suspended, he still hadn't been found guilty of any crimes—nor, for that matter, was he ever likely to be.

"He's here...?" Claudia wiped the sweat from her brow as she looked up to fully take in the undecorated two-story mansion.

At first glance, it looked like any other typical mansion, but on closer inspection, there were all kinds of security devices installed amid the flowering garden, and the premises were under twenty-four-hour surveillance by Galaxy's private military forces. There were no other inhabitants on the island, and it was forbidden for outsiders to even approach the landmass without explicit clearance.

"Come now, Claudia." Isabella, her expression cool, entered the building ahead of her.

Claudia breathed a sigh of relief to find that it was air-conditioned on the inside but couldn't help but feel as if someone was watching her—no doubt because the security cameras had been arranged so as not to leave a single blind spot.

Even so, Ladislav's circumstances looked to be much more comfortable than she had imagined. By the looks of things, he was afforded a certain degree of freedom so long as he complied with the rules. She had imagined that he would have been locked away in a tiny, dirty cell, but to her surprise, that wasn't the case.

Then again, Galaxy hadn't confined him here just for possessing secrets of the highest order—even if he was the chief party involved in those secrets—but rather because of the threat posed by Varda. Claudia didn't know the details, but it sounded like if he wasn't dealt with appropriately, he, or maybe Varda, might expose all kinds of information. Faced with all this, even Galaxy would have no choice but to accommodate him to a certain extent.

Claudia followed her mother to the second floor, where they found an old man sitting in a shaded wicker chair on the balcony.

"How long has it been, professor?" Isabella called out in greeting.

The man, shrunken and frail like a withered old tree, turned sluggishly toward them. "...Don't call me that. You'll make this old fool cry, reminding me of everything I've lost. I'm not a professor anymore."

Just looking at his eyes, Claudia could see right away he wasn't in a good state—physically or mentally.

*Ahh, this is no good.*

They were stagnant, completely sapped of all vitality, the eyes of someone who had already given up on life, who now lived only in the past.

If he had been detained here ever since the Jade Twilight Incident, then he must have been living like this for over thirty years. That meant he would have to be in his eighties. This genius, who had single-handedly advanced Orga Lux research by more than half a century, whose creations included the Varda-Vaos, the Pan-Dora, and the Lyre-Poros, and whom Saya had described as so significant that his name would probably be remembered throughout history, had been unable to resist the passage of time.

"How long has it been since I last spoke to anyone...? What do you want?" Only then did Ladislav seem to notice Claudia. "Oh, you have a young lady with you...from Seidoukan, judging by the uniform. That brings back memories."

"Pleased to meet you, professor. My name is Claudia Enfield," she introduced herself, before taking the Pan-Dora from the holder at her waist, activating it. "I'm currently this one's partner."

"Ah, Pan-Dora, is it? She was always the most difficult of my children. She'll give you trouble, I'm sure."

"Oh, she already has."

Ladislav nodded, smiling fondly.

He seemed to be looking far into the distance, through both Claudia and the Orga Lux, no doubt deep into the past.

"I'd like to ask you about the *true nature* of this one's abilities."

"...!" At this, Ladislav's eyes opened wide. "Its true nature, you say...?"

Isabella, standing beside her daughter, frowned with suspicion.

"The Pan-Dora's true ability isn't precognition. That's merely a by-product, isn't it?"

"Oh-ho...!" Ladislav rose up from his chair, his eyes suddenly returning to life as he approached her on unsteady feet.

"Marvelous…! To think… To think that someone would reach this stage… I'd long since given up hope…"

"…So I was right."

She could no doubt take his reaction as proof of the validity of her assumptions.

It was vital to have the right frame of mind when using an Orga Lux. While there were many who thought that they understood that, it meant a lot more than most realized.

"Then its real cost…"

"Ha-ha, you already know the answer to that, I'm sure."

"…is the future itself. No?"

"…!" Isabella's frown stiffened, but Ladislav, in contrast, broke into a wide grin, taking Claudia by the hand.

"Claudia, was it? Thanks to you, I can die knowing I've brought more successes into this world than just the Varda-Vaos. When the Lyre-Poros was downgraded, I couldn't help but think that I'd failed, but now…"

"No, I should be thanking you, professor. You've lifted a burden from my shoulders."

The question now was what to do next.

If there really was such a thing as fate, then there must have been some reason why she had survived this far.

"Ah, I haven't felt this good in a long time… Ah yes, Isabella. I wasn't going to tell you, but I want to thank you for bringing me this news, so I will. The Varda-Vaos dropped by the other day."

"…Is that so?" Isabella's voice was cold and mechanical. Due to the mental adjustment programs that she had undertaken, her thought processes would become emotionless and calculating whenever serious issues affecting Galaxy came up. "Tell me."

"Oh, we didn't talk about anything too serious. She was just worried about me. She needs me, in case anything was to happen to her, you see. No one else understands her makeup the way I do. She's had others do maintenance on her, but if she ever ended up getting broken, well now, there's no one else in this world capable of fixing her."

"What did you discuss with her?" Isabella asked dispassionately.

Ladislav shrugged his shoulders. "She asked me whether there were any others. People close to reaching the world that I began to peer into."

"And what did you say?"

"Oh, that as far as the published papers I've read go—and I haven't received any new ones for a while now, you know—there's only two names that come to mind."

Needless to say, Ladislav didn't have any research facilities at his disposal, but it sounded like he was permitted to stay abreast of the work of others.

"There's a chance that Ernesta Kühne and Hilda Jane Rowlands could make it. That's what I told her."

"And did the Varda-Vaos want anything else?"

"That was all. She left straight afterward. A particularly undevoted daughter, that one." Ladislav laughed from the back of his throat, returning to his wicker chair. "I hope this old body of mine can hold out long enough to see what she's set her mind to..."

"Claudia. We're leaving," Isabella announced, her voice scraped clean of all emotion, as she turned her back on the balcony and the throaty laughter of the old scientist.

# CHAPTER 5
# THE TOUDOU
# HOUSEHOLD

The head school of the Toudou style was presently based in Sendai, though the residence was located in a hilly area to the west of the city. Ayato and Kirin arrived outside the grand complex just as petals of snow began to flutter down from the clouds above.

There were several large buildings in the Sukiya-zukuri architectural style throughout the grounds, and many others that from outside looked like dojos. It would be easy to mistake it all for the palatial compound of a feudal lord from the Edo period.

"This is, how do I put it...? Impressive..." Ayato, passing under the simple yet dignified front gate as they made their way to the main residence, was struck with admiration.

While it was fair to say that his own house, being fitted with a dojo, also occupied a large area, this was on a totally different level—although, to be fair, it was presumptuous even to compare the two, seeing as the Amagiri Shinmei style wasn't presently taking any students, while the Toudou style had more than ten thousand scattered across countless branches throughout the world.

"No... It's too big to live comfortably in, really." Kirin glanced down, embarrassed, only lifting her head as they approached the entrance of what looked like the main building.

She took a long, deep breath, before opening the door and calling out: "I'm home!"

"Ah, welcome back!" came a hoarse though dignified voice.

Glancing over Kirin's shoulder, Ayato saw an old woman standing in the center of the grand entryway.

"Great-aunt, I'm sorry for not calling in so long."

"You sure took your time. That Rikka isn't all that far away, you know. You could pay to stop in a little more often."

Her white hair tied up in a bun, she was a short woman, wearing what Ayato could tell at first glance was an expensive *tsumugi* kimono. She looked to be of advanced years, with deep wrinkles engraved into her face, but her posture was rigid and straight, like that of a tempered blade.

"And you…you would be Ayato Amagiri, I see."

"Pleased to meet you. Thank you for letting me visit at such short notice."

"It *is* short notice; there's no arguing there, but we *did* invite you. I'm Yoshino Agatsuma. I may have only married into one of the branch families, but now I represent the interests of the head family." She had a curt manner of speaking, but her lips curled up in a warm smile. "But this is no place to talk. Come in."

Yoshino led them down a corridor so long that Ayato couldn't even count how many rooms filled the house.

From the passageway, he could see various courtyards and gardens nestled among the buildings, each of them meticulously kept. A place the size of the Amagiri household required considerable effort to maintain, but there was no way that a family, no matter how large it might be, could take care of an estate of this size alone. Indeed, every now and then he caught sight of people sweeping the pavements or tending to the plants. Whenever they saw Yoshino or Kirin, they would stop what they were doing and bow respectfully toward them.

"They're all students here. We're in the middle of a big cleanup for the end of the year."

There were several rows of what looked like student domiciles situated behind the dojos, so there were probably a considerable number of disciples who lived on the grounds.

Of course, such students would normally be entrusted to a branch dojo where they would receive initial training from more advanced disciples, but with Kirin's performance in the Phoenix and the Gryps, the deluge of prospective applicants eager to learn the Toudou style must have been pushing them to capacity.

"That said, being the end of the year, many of them have gone back to their families. Heaven alone knows whether we'll be able to get everything finished today..."

"Ah...!" Kirin, walking along beside him, came to a sudden stop.

Her eyes became teary, a look of joy spreading across her face.

In front of her stood a man. He looked to be in his forties, if Ayato had to guess, of slender build and tall stature, neatly dressed in a loose, casual kimono, and he had a gentle smile on his face.

"Welcome home... Although, it probably sounds strange, me saying that. I guess I'm the one's who's back."

"Dad!" As if she could wait no longer, Kirin ran forward, leaping into his arms.

So this was Seijirou Toudou. From what Kirin had told him, Ayato had assumed that he would be rather strict but the figure tenderly holding his daughter and lovingly stroking her head could hardly be further from that image.

"...We have you and your friends to thank. We're in your debt," Yoshino said, patting Ayato on the back.

Yoshino said little, but her affection for Kirin and Seijirou came through in her voice.

"No, Kirin did it herself."

"Is that so? I'm glad to hear you say that, and yet... It looks like she still has some way to go." Yoshino let out a brief sigh, her countenance and tone of voice suddenly intensifying. "Kirin! Not in front of our guest!"

"Ah... S-sorry...!" Kirin froze for a moment, her gaze darting back and forth, before letting go of her father and stepping back to a respectful distance.

Try as she might, however, she couldn't hide the joy that had spread across her face. Nor did Yoshino reprove her for it.

*What a nice family...*

Ayato could practically feel the warmth radiating out from them.

Ayato and Kirin sat formally across from Yoshino and Seijirou inside a room that, at roughly thirteen feet wide, was too big for him to feel truly at ease.

"I apologize for the delay. I'm Seijirou Toudou, Kirin's father."

"Ayato Amagiri."

Still kneeling, the two of them bowed to each other politely.

"My daughter has told me all about you, Mr. Amagiri. Thank you for looking after her...and me, too." Only then did Seijirou raise his face to look directly at him.

"As I said in my letter, we all entered the Gryps hoping to have our own wishes granted, and our victory was only possible thanks to everyone's efforts," Ayato explained. "If you want to thank us for helping Kirin get hers, then we all need to thank her, too, for helping grant ours. We couldn't have done it without her."

Strictly speaking, Saya had entered the tournament for a different reason, but there was no need for him to overcomplicate things now.

"I see... You're right, of course. But still, I want to express my deepest thanks," Seijirou answered, bowing once more.

As awkward as it made him feel, if Kirin's father wanted to thank him this much, Ayato wouldn't try to stop him.

Seijirou remained that way for a full ten seconds before looking up.

"Well then," Yoshino began, "let's get down to business. I'd like to hear your answer, Kirin."

At the sound of these words, the atmosphere suddenly turned tense.

She was no doubt referring to her suggestion that Kirin return home and take over as head of the main branch of the Toudou school.

Thanks to having met Masatsugu, Kirin seemed to have overcome her indecision, but Ayato still didn't know what exactly she had decided.

He could feel his hands growing sweaty as he waited for her to respond.

He would respect her choice, no matter what it was, but there was no denying that he would be devastated if she decided not to come back to Asterisk.

"...I'm not ready yet," she began, glancing toward Ayato. "I realized the other day that it's presumptuous of someone as young as me to even worry about where to go with my swordsmanship. It's a journey without end, and I'm still only just at the beginning of it. So I don't think I'll be able to guide others yet. I'd like to go back to Asterisk and learn more."

Hearing this, Ayato felt a wave of relief wash over him.

At the very least, Kirin herself wanted to stay at Seidoukan.

"Hmm, I don't know what to say...," Yoshino said. "I think we would all agree that you're the most advanced user of the Toudou style. Neither I nor Seijirou have mastered the Conjoined Cranes quite like you have... No, even looking further back, no one else has been able to reach the level of our founder quite like you have. There's no one else more suited to the role than you."

Kirin shook her head. "No. Maybe I'm a fast learner, but that's all there is to it."

"...Are you saying that all that effort you put into your learning had nothing to do with it?" Yoshino, wearing a somewhat contrived smile, looked toward her.

Faced with that sharp gaze, Kirin's voice fell quiet. "I think people's personalities come through in their use of the sword. So a teacher needs to be ready for that. Even if my techniques are as good as you say, that's just raw strength... I'm not trying to be modest, but that isn't what lies at the heart of the way of the sword."

"Oh? Then what does?"

"…Conviction… Backed up by experience."

"Conviction?" Yoshino repeated in a low voice.

"By continuously facing one's sword, by cultivating one's inner self," Kirin answered decisively.

"I see. And you have to return to Rikka to do that?"

For the first time, a shadow of doubt fell over Kirin's face, and she dropped her gaze. "…To be honest, I don't know. There are things that people can learn by themselves, and yet…" She paused there, falling silent for a long, drawn-out moment, before finally continuing. "And yet, as I am now… I've only improved as much as I have thanks to being able to fight alongside my friends. So I'd like to stay there a little longer." Only now did she raise her head, her gaze meeting Yoshino's. "If the way of the sword is a journey without end, then even if it takes me more time to come back here, it shouldn't make too much difference over the long term."

"…"

Yoshino stared at Kirin in silence for what felt like an eternity, before finally letting out a small sigh, her expression loosening. "Over the long term… You say that so easily. I'm at an age where I can't count on my final calling holding back till I'm ready…"

"G-Great-aunt!"

Yoshino, however, stared back at her flustered niece gently, seemingly holding back a flood of laughter. "Don't worry about that. But if you had thought it over properly yourself, you probably wouldn't have needed to ask others for advice."

"—! B-but—"

"Well, I suppose we can try to make it work. Isn't that right, Seijirou?"

"…Yes." Seijirou, too, looked as if he were holding back a smile.

"But if that's how it is, then I guess I can't afford to kick the bucket for a while yet." Yoshino tiredly rubbed her shoulders, before flashing Kirin an amused smile.

"Th-thank you, great-aunt!"

\*

For Julis, the redevelopment area wasn't a place of fond memories.

Whether it was the incident with Silas, or her reunion with Orphelia, this part of the city had only ever given her trouble.

She would have preferred never to have to bother with it all again. Now, however, she had found herself once again setting foot there.

"...Where exactly are you taking me, Lester?" she asked cautiously.

The sun had already set, and their surroundings were veiled in deep darkness.

There were no streetlamps in the redevelopment area. Their only sources of light were the torch that Lester held in front of him and the flame that Julis had summoned through her abilities.

"You want to know what I've been doing this past month, right? So shut up and follow me. I can't *tell* you, so I'll have to *show* you."

This would be the perfect opportunity to set a trap, Julis thought, but at least with Lester, she could be sure that he wouldn't succumb to such underhanded methods.

The wintry wind snipping at her body and the distinct dust-filled air of the redevelopment area both seemed to be urging to her turn around and go back, but she wasn't about to let them get in the way of finding out how Lester had improved so dramatically in so short a time.

Lester came to a stop in front of an abandoned building at the end of the street, seemingly no different in appearance from every other structure they had passed to reach it.

"Here," Lester said brusquely.

He made his way to the entrance, moonlight shining in through the broken roof above him, as he took something from his pocket.

"What's that?" Julis asked.

"My pass," Lester replied with a daring smile as he showed it to her.

It was a seal, skillfully designed though small enough to fit in the palm of one's hand, depicting a motif in vivid green of what looked like a kingfisher.

It began to let off a faint light, when—

"Huh?!"

Brilliant lines of light suddenly shot through the air around them, rearranging before them like some kind of puzzle. When Julis's senses returned, she was standing in the center of a spacious hall.

"What was...?"

No matter which direction she looked, there were no walls in sight, only the wooden floor continuing without end. The space was lit by countless candle-like lights floating around them, but there were no actual candles to speak of.

It was a boundless, tranquil space.

"Oh-ho! I see you've brought a friend with you this time, Lester!"

Julis spun around at the sound of that childish, innocent voice echoing through the room.

Behind her stood a young girl, her hair done up in a butterfly-like bun.

"Ban'yuu Tenra...!"

The girl was none other than Jie Long Seventh Institute's top-ranked fighter and student council president, Xinglou Fan.

Julis recognized her immediately from their semifinal match at the Gryps, though she had never before spoken to her in person.

"Welcome, Glühen Rose... Although, I thought you weren't supposed to tell anyone about this place," she said, turning toward Lester with a dangerous glint in her eyes.

"Hmph, I *didn't* tell her. She followed me here herself," Lester began defensively, when—

"*Gah?!*"

Xinglou threw him across the room with the palm of her hand.

He plummeted through the air like a giant doll, landing hard on the floor before he could so much as brace himself for the impact.

"I'll forgive you this time, but let that be a lesson for you. There will be no second chances."

"Nngh...! Why you...!" Lester spat out, before losing consciousness and falling flat on his face.

"What an annoyance," Xinglou said, turning to Julis. "I suppose he got impatient and challenged you to a duel? I did tell him that he would need another six months before he could hope to match you."

"...Looks like I was right. You *were* the one behind him."

Xinglou Fan was well-known even at Seidoukan. Everyone knew that all her eleven fellow Page Ones at Jie Long trained under her guidance.

On top of that, if her training was anything like what Julis had just witnessed, that went some way toward explaining Lester's mental growth as well.

"Indeed. Although, he isn't one of my disciples. I simply thought to help draw out his potential."

"But why would Jie Long's top fighter want to help train a Page One from Seidoukan?" Julis asked cautiously.

No matter how she tried to look at it, it didn't make any sense, and yet there had to be some kind of reasoning behind it.

"Oh-ho-ho, it isn't only Seidoukan," Xinglou answered indifferently, as if she had nothing to do with it.

"Huh...?"

As Xinglou waved her hand, several large images floated up before them.

They resembled air-windows, but Xinglou carried nothing that could have switched them on, nor did there seem to be any projectors installed throughout the hall.

But more important than whatever technology or ability Xinglou had at her disposal were the various faces that she saw before her.

"Irene Urzaiz. And her sister, too..."

One of the images showed the two sisters whom Julis and Ayato had fought during the Phoenix. She had never guessed that the two of them could have become Xinglou's playthings.

"The younger one merely came free with the sister. Incidentally, these aren't recordings. This is them as they are right now."

"What? Then how are you...?"

Xinglou merely responded to her question with a wordless laugh.

Julis turned back to the other images, each of them depicting students whom Julis could easily guess would be more than willing to fight Xinglou.

"That's Overliezel and Kennin Fubatsu from Queenvale... And Allekant's Ningirsu... And Perceforêt from Gallardworth..."

In other words, there were students there from all six of Asterisk's schools.

"Don't tell me you're training all of them?"

"I don't spoon-feed them, if that's what you mean. I've had my eye on all of them for quite some time, Lester included. I hadn't intended to begin in earnest until the new year, but then I found I couldn't hold myself back. When we get started properly, we should have around three times this number... Close to twenty, I'd say." Xinglou puffed out her chest in pride, a chilling smile rising to her lips. "I desire strong fighters—strong enough to make my blood seethe with excitement."

"...So you can fight them yourself?"

Xinglou Fan's extraordinary love for battle was near legendary.

"Indeed." She nodded simply.

"I see. But in that case...maybe this isn't for me to say, but it doesn't look like you have any top-class fighters among them."

The faces projected before her all belonged to ranked students. There was no doubting their ability, at least in that regard, and yet—there were none among them of particularly outstanding characteristics, certainly no one like Orphelia Landlufen, Xiaohui Wu, or even, for that matter, Ayato or Kirin.

"Indeed!" Xinglou leaned forward, her eyes sparkling with delight at this observation. "In the past, I cared only for those of spectacular natural abilities... But then I realized that it was those with more warped talents who were most capable of overcoming the barriers that I desire. All those that I have gathered here have such potential... Dear me! Even at my age, there's still so much to learn."

"Overcoming barriers...," Julis repeated.

If that was indeed possible, then—

"Of course, I would like to give shape to something resembling Ayato Amagiri, but that won't be easy with these materials. It will take effort to mold these ones, and time away from Jie Long." Xinglou breathed a disappointed sigh. "And I hardly think the other schools, or indeed their integrated enterprise foundations, would look too warmly on my efforts. Not that that bothers me, but who knows what that will do to Rikka? I do so adore this city."

"...Ban'yuu Tenra."

"Yes?"

Julis had made up her mind. "Can you add me? Just like the others?"

"Oh...?" Xinglou narrowed her eyes in delight.

No matter what, Julis was determined to defeat Orphelia. To that end, she was willing to do whatever it took.

If Xinglou were able to help her...if that would enable her to overcome the barriers that held her back, she would gladly submit herself to her.

And yet—

"I'm afraid not."

"What?!" Julis demanded. "Why not?! Are you saying I'm not good enough for you?"

Xinglou, however, gave her a regretful look. "Quite the opposite. I think very highly of you. I could devour you this very moment, in fact. If you'll let me use a little example that I've become fond of, you're like a mixed gemstone. One of particularly high quality. Even now, the only people in this city capable of facing you are those who have already overcome their barriers."

"Then why—"

"But you've already maximized your potential. If you're a gemstone, then you've already been polished till you gleam. Unfortunate though it is, there's nothing left for me to mold."

"What?!"

But Julis herself had felt the same way for some time now.

No matter how much effort she put into her training, she doubted she would be able to reach the level of Ayato or Kirin. She thought she had understood that, but hearing it put into words was too much of a shock.

"...I see. So there are barriers that I *can't* overcome."

"Regrettably—"

"But I can't give up now!" Julis said, as if trying to convince herself, as she forced her eyes shut.

Reality was cruel. If she couldn't achieve what she wanted through ordinary means, then she would have to try something more drastic.

In a way, Xinglou's refusal to teach her had only strengthened her resolve.

As she was now, she wouldn't be able to win the Lindvolus...or save Orphelia.

"In the name of the unyielding Red Lotus, I, Julis-Alexia von Riessfeld, challenge thee, Xinglou Fan, to a duel!" she declared as she readied her school crest.

Xinglou's mouth opened wide in delight, her eyes sparkling with curiosity. "Oh-ho! Now you *have* surprised me. But are you sure you haven't lost your mind?"

"...Come at me with everything you've got. Then you can ask me that again."

There was no way that Julis would actually be able to defeat Xinglou. She had known that from the beginning. She could sense the overwhelming power of the young woman standing across from her just by looking at her.

"Very well. You didn't think I would turn you down, did you?" Xinglou said, raising her hand to her own school crest to accept the challenge.

"...Let me ask you one thing first," Julis said, holding up a finger as the automated voice opened the duel.

"And what would that be?"

"If you were to fight Orphelia, who would win?"

At this question, Xinglou crossed her arms, deep in thought. "That's a difficult one... Yes, that girl grows stronger by the day... If we were to fight now, it would be me. Although, if we waited until the Festa, who knows?"

"I see... That's good enough." Julis nodded, before activating her Rect Lux and deploying its remote units around her. "I'll adjust my fighting style based on what you just said, Ban'yuu Tenra... Knowing you, you'll survive."

"Oh? I'm afraid I don't have the slightest clue what you're talking about, but if you're ready, let's begin."

No sooner did Xinglou, her excitement written large on her face, finish speaking than a crushing sense of dominance began to emanate from the Ban'yuu Tenra's whole body—so strong that Julis couldn't help but feel that, were her focus to waver, the pressure alone would be enough to knock her unconscious.

This was an opponent against whom, under any normal circumstances, she would have no chance of holding her ground.

But that was precisely why she had challenged her. She had to try.

She knew what she had to do, at least in theory. She only had to put it into practice.

Julis channeled every ounce of her concentration on forming the image in her mind, increasing her prana as she quietly murmured: "Flourish—*Queen of the Night!*"

∗

Lester awoke to a strong burning sensation, only to the find the floorboards of the space around him completely burned away.

"Wh-what the...?" He leaped to his feet, but fortunately, he seemed to have escaped unscathed.

He glanced around at the now-exposed earth until he located Xinglou, her uniform badly scorched, and Julis, her breathing ragged, having fallen to her knees.

At her feet lay her broken Red Lotus school crest.

"...Gwa-ha-ha-ha!" Xinglou's laughter, rich and sonorant, was nothing if not genuine. "That was quite unimaginable! How many centuries has it been since I met someone as crazy as you?" She rested her hands on her hips. "Do you realize that if you had made even the slightest mistake there, you may well have lost your life?"

"Haah... Haah..." Julis, on the other hand, her burnt clothes revealing countless defensive charms attached to her body, wore an undaunted grin. "I know... But a Strega's power lies in her will and her ability to imagine her creations... I wouldn't mess that up."

"Oh? What makes you so sure?"

"Because I can't afford to die until I've saved Orphelia...!" she declared.

The charms, their power spent, suddenly burned away in a brilliant flash.

A number of fresh charms suddenly appeared in Xinglou's hand, before flying through the air to attach themselves to Julis.

"Hmm, that's easy enough to say... You've caught my interest, Glühen Rose." Xinglou rested her hand on Julis's jaw, tilting her head upward to stare into her eyes. "You can forget what I said before. I want to be there to see just how far you can go."

"In that case—"

"However!" Xinglou thrust her hand toward Julis, as if to rein in the joy that now flashed in her eyes. "There are several conditions if you want my training. First, I'm not here to grant you techniques or power. You will push yourself through battle, until you find them for yourself."

"...I understand." Julis nodded obediently.

"Taking into account the burden it will put on your body, the door leading here will open for you only once a week. The entrance will be different each time. This arrangement will last until the Lindvolus. That is the goal most of those whom I have invited here are aiming for. As I said to Lester, you breathe not a word of this to anyone."

Julis nodded once more.

"And finally… When we're finished, you will fight me at my full strength."

Julis startled at this last condition.

"Fret not. I'm no demon. I'll be looking forward to the end of the tournament," Xinglou said, smiling down at her.

"Agreed," Julis answered without the slightest hesitation. "I accept your conditions."

"Excellent! Then I shall gladly welcome you to my private school, the Liangshan!"

# CHAPTER 6
# FAMILY TIES

"Phew… So that's that." Ayato wiped the sweat from his brow as he looked back at the freshly cleaned corridor, nodding in satisfaction at the dull luster of the aged floorboards.

He'd been cleaning dojos ever since his childhood, but when it was someone else's house, he couldn't just do it however he pleased, nor set about it half-heartedly. As he was in the middle of double-checking that he hadn't missed anything, Kirin came all but skipping down the hallway.

"Ah, um, thank you, Ayato. We shouldn't be making you do so much this, being a guest and all."

"No, it's okay. You helped me and my dad out at my place, and besides, I'm the one who's making a nuisance of myself on New Year's Eve… Who's that?" Ayato turned his gaze toward the woman he noticed standing behind her.

She was a full head taller than Kirin, with remarkably similar features. Her lustrous, black hair was tied back with a clasp, her neat, white sweater hiding a bosom that rivaled Kirin's own. No doubt seeing his confusion, she broke out into a friendly grin.

"Nice to meet you, Ayato. I'm Kirin's mother, Kotoha."

"Huh?! Ah, um, my apologies! Pleased to meet you! I'm Ayato Amagiri!" Flustered, he hurried to hide the cleaning cloth still grasped in his hand, and adopted a formal kneeling position, head bowed.

"There's no need to stand on ceremony." Kotoha laughed. "From what I hear, you're always looking out for my girl here. Thank you."

Ayato could hardly hold back his surprise. While Saya's mother, Kaya, also looked young for her age, Kotoha would easily have been able pass for Kirin's older sister. On top of that, her general aura and relaxed manner were completely at odds with the almost martial characters of Seijirou and Yoshino.

"U-um, Mom isn't a Genestella, and she can't really…well, I don't think she's ever even held a sword."

"Ah, I see." Ayato nodded in understanding.

"It's true. I simply married into a wealthy family," Kotoha said with a broad smile.

For a second, Ayato had thought she was joking, but to his surprise, she was completely serious.

"Ah, but I did learn all kinds of things before entering the family, like how to cook, how to wash and clean and so forth… I'm still learning, though, so I guess I've still got a ways to go."

Ayato startled at her use of the word *still*. Just how long had she been doing this?

Even assuming that she had given birth to Kirin only shortly after marrying, she would still have to have been part of the family for at least fifteen years by now.

"Um…"

"Oh, uh, my mom… She has a very relaxed personality. Not that she isn't afraid of anything, it's more like she tends to say whatever comes to mind…," Kirin whispered under her breath, looking slightly embarrassed.

"…I see."

She sounded like the exact opposite of her daughter personality-wise.

"But…she's probably the strongest member of the family."

"Huh?"

"She's got a strong will, I guess you could say... When Dad was imprisoned, she was the one who took it the calmest."

"Oh...?"

That came as something of a surprise.

"She trusts everyone, from the bottom of her heart."

"I see. She sounds like a wonderful mother."

"And what are you two whispering about? Let Mom in!" Kotoha beamed, suddenly embracing the both of them in her arms.

"Wha—?!"

"Mom!"

Her embrace not being an attack, of course, Ayato had been taken by complete surprise. Both he and Kirin were at her mercy.

"M-Mom, please...!" Kirin protested weakly, her face turning bright red, but Kotoha didn't seem to have noticed.

Ayato, feeling his arm caught up against Kirin's breast, reflexively tried to pull away, but Kotoha, perhaps sensing his movements, only held on all the tighter, until he could feel her breasts, too, pushing against his back.

"M-Mom! That's enough!" Kirin exclaimed as she gently pushed her mother back.

Ayato breathed a sigh of relief.

"Heh-heh, look at you, Kirin." Kotoha laughed with a gentle smile. "Ah, youth is so wonderful, isn't it? You should try flirting with him a bit more."

"Fl-flirting...?!" Kirin's face, already scarlet, turned darker still—to the point where Ayato wouldn't have been surprised to see steam rising from her head. "M-Mom! Ayato and I don't... I mean...!"

"Oh? But I thought you liked him?"

"Wha—?!" Kirin blurted out, her body turning rigid. "Wh-wh-what are y-y-you...?!"

"And I heard you went to greet his father yesterday. Right, Ayato?"

"Huh? Um, well, I don't know if *greet* is the right word..." But he couldn't help but shrink back at the force of her excitement, and he could do nothing but nod along weakly.

"And now you've brought Ayato here! You're asking for permission from both families, right?" Kotoha clapped her hands together in excitement. "That's it, we should arrange the engagement right away! Everything's fine by me, and I'm sure your father won't have any objections!"

"E-e-e-engagement?!" Kirin, unable to properly articulate herself, stepped backward, her eyes darting in every possible direction.

"You're a late bloomer, Kirin, and if you don't act now, someone else might snatch him up first. And look, Ayato here is already... Huh?" Kotoha suddenly fell silent, before bringing her face startlingly close to his own and staring deep into his eyes.

"I-is something wrong?"

"No... Heh-heh, there's something about you that reminds me of someone I used to know... Your eyes and bearing are practically identical." Kotoha let out a light chuckle, but a sad look had taken root in her gaze.

"Someone you used to know...?"

"Oh? A friend of mine... She passed away a long time ago."

"Oh... I'm sorry," Ayato apologized.

"Don't worry about it," Kotoha said with a wave of her hand. "It was back when I was a student. But she was a Genestella, you see, and very strong at that. Right... She took part in that thing you and Kirin fought in, the one where you paired up... What was it called again...?"

"...The Phoenix?" Kirin asked. She had managed to calm herself down, but her face was still tinged red.

"Right, right!" Kotoha nodded forcefully, almost as if she were the child. "She even managed to win it, that Phoenix tournament! Every single match!"

If that was true, then this friend of hers must certainly have been strong.

Perhaps it was presumptuous of him to think so, but from Ayato's experience, no normal fighter could hope to win the Festa.

"What was her name...?" he asked cautiously.

"Akari," Kotoha answered, as if looking back fondly on the distant past. "Akari Yachigusa."

Unfortunately, Ayato hadn't heard the name before, but there was still something about it that struck a chord.

"Yachigusa…," Kirin repeated. "You mean…?"

"Right, *that* Yachigusa family."

"Kirin, do you know them?" Ayato asked.

"Yes." She nodded. "Mom's family has dealings with them every now and then. I've met a few of them myself. It's just…" Kirin paused there, her expression clouding over.

"Ah, they probably didn't leave a very good impression… Maybe it's because they're such an old house, set in their ways, but they're not particularly fond of Genestella…"

Even today, prejudice against Genestella was still rife around the world—and in Japan in particular.

"Akari was such a delicate, gentle person and so beautiful that even I might have fallen in love with her… A truly wonderful girl. Maybe Kirin takes after me there, what with her being so charmed by you. You do so resemble her!"

"M-Mom! I just…," Kirin stammered, yanking her mother's arm in an attempt to pull her away.

"Here you are, Kirin," came a familiar voice echoing down the hallway, followed by the sound of footsteps.

"You…!"

"Ayato Amagiri? What are you doing here…?" Standing across from them was a well-built middle-aged man dressed in a tidy suit—Kirin's uncle, Kouichirou.

"U-Uncle! I'm sorry I haven't called in so long!" Kirin stammered, hurriedly lowering her head out of respect.

"Ah, Kou. Welcome back."

"Kou…?" Kouichirou appeared a little taken aback by Kotoha's laid-back attitude for a brief moment but quickly cleared his throat, turning toward Kirin. "Ahem! Kirin, I need to have a word with you. Follow me."

"Y-yes!" Kirin glanced toward Ayato, before doing as told.

"…" Meanwhile, Ayato continued to stare at the older man in silence.

"Don't worry," Kouichirou said, as if having sensed his unease. "I don't hold it against you."

"Huh...?"

The older man's voice was calmer than Ayato remembered, devoid of the harsh edge it had once carried.

As they watched the two of them disappear down the corridor, Kotoha let out a light chuckle. "It looks like Kou's finally come back to his old self."

*

Kirin and Kouichirou had gone to a room deep in the expansive Toudou household.

"Starting today, it's been decided that I'll come back to the main house," Kouichirou said over a cup of tea a student had brought in.

"Huh...?" Kirin opened her eyes wide in surprise at the unexpected announcement.

Kouichirou had decided to leave the Toudou family back when Seijirou had been selected instead of him to succeed as head, and he had essentially cut all ties with them. Perhaps he had had a change of heart, Kirin wondered, but even so, simply coming back after all that time wouldn't be so easy. To begin with, there would certainly be conditions he would be expected to fulfill.

"Aunt Yoshino asked me directly. She's decided to put me in charge of general management and the overseas branches."

"Great-aunt did...?"

As the acting head, Yoshino's word was more or less law.

"But what about your work at Galaxy?"

"I've already resigned. The handover took longer than I was hoping, though."

"What?!"

Once someone secured a position at Galaxy's headquarters, they entered the realm of the ultra-elite. No matter how strongly one might want to, it was all but impossible to step back from such lofty heights. The only way out was normally an ungraceful one, usually the result of in-house rivalry.

"Does that mean... Was it my fault?"

Kouichirou had tried to use Kirin as a tool for his own career advancement, but there was an advantage to be had from her perspective, too. She didn't regret leaving his side, but if not for him, she would never have been able to advance all the way to the Festa, let alone emerge victorious, so she couldn't help but feel as if she had somehow failed him.

"Don't flatter yourself. You had nothing to do with this," he rebuked her. "I simply realized my role in things and decided accordingly." He paused there to take another mouthful of his tea. "And besides, I watched your performance in the semifinal. What on earth were you thinking?"

"I—I'm sorry..."

There was no mistaking that it had been Kirin who had secured her team's victory during that match, but it was also true that her actions had left her so badly injured that she had been unable to participate in the final. The skill and power of her opponent, Xiaohui Wu, had exceeded her own in every respect, and he had been able to run circles around her until the very last second.

"Not only that, but you even managed to destroy the Senbakiri..."

"Ah..." Kirin had no response to that.

The Senbakiri had been passed down in the Toudou family for generations and possessed a value that couldn't be measured in money alone. There was no one to blame for its loss but herself.

"Honestly, you're still no more than a child. You won't have any future waiting for you if you don't stop and think about just how much danger that way of fighting put you in." Kouichirou paused there, his expression remaining sullen as he reached for a large wooden box leaning against the wall behind him, before thrusting it toward her.

"Uncle... What's this?"

"..." Kouichirou merely closed his eyes, not deigning to respond to her question.

All she could do was untie the cord wrapped around it.

"—! This is…!"

"The Hiinamaru, forged by the ancient swordsmith Kunikane Youkei."

Inside the box lay a Japanese katana. The steel was clearly of an exceptionally high quality, terribly sharp and with a glowing polish, while the border between the hardened and unhardened portions was of indescribable beauty.

"It's yours. Use it," Kouichirou said brusquely.

"B-but this, this is…!"

The Hiinamaru was the Toudou family's greatest treasure, and it had been given to Kouichirou to make up for the fact that his younger brother, Seijirou, had been selected over him to become head of the family. Kouichirou had taken it with him when he left.

"You're the future of the Toudou style. And besides, I can't hold onto that thing forever."

Despite what he said, Kouichirou very well could have kept it for himself or sold it—or done literally anything else with it.

And yet, he was giving it to her.

There was meaning in that action. Kirin could feel the heat of his gaze upon her.

"…Thank you," she said in a thin voice.

Kouichirou, seemingly embarrassed, averted his gaze. "Hmph." He snorted. "So I'm finally freed from Dad's 'compassion.' Talk about a relief."

Kirin, however, could sense the hurt that lay beneath his words.

*

The guestroom to which Ayato had been shown was much larger than the one at his own house.

To be honest, he couldn't bring himself to relax in it.

"So I spent the last New Year's at Julis's house…or palace, I guess. And this one at Kirin's…"

He didn't normally dwell too deeply on the turning of the years, but this time around, he couldn't help but feel a tinge of unease.

What would the next one hold? Or the year after that? Or the one after that?

Would Haruka be there with him?

As he was mulling over these questions, his mobile began to ring. The caller's name was hidden.

A bad feeling had fallen over him even before he could open the air-window.

"*Kee-hee-hee-hee! Greetings, Ayato Amagiri,*" came a familiar dry, rasping laugh. "*Has it already been a year?*" That face in the air-window, with its droopy, upturned eyes and large glasses, broke out into a lopsided grin.

Ayato couldn't say that he hadn't been expecting this call.

"…What do you want, Magnum Opus?"

"*I wanted to congratulate you on winning the tournament, of course, although I'll admit I'm a little late.*" Hilda broke into laughter once more, her eyes narrowing like a cat's. "*Exactly as I had predicted. You really were splendid—absolutely marvelous. I can't tell you how delighted I am to be talking to the champion of not only the Phoenix, but the Gryps, too… Incidentally, how is your wish coming along?*"

"So that's what this is about. Are you in a hurry?"

"*No hurry at all. I just thought that you might have reconsidered by now.*" Hilda shone him a knowing smirk, almost as if trying to hint at something. "*You've already heard from that creep of an executive chairman, I take it? I'm the only one who can wake your sister. So come now, unshackle me and I'll give you what you want.*"

"…You're not the only option. Director Korbel might have found a way."

"*Kee-hee-hee-hee! There's no need to play hard to get. If you're willing to wait several decades, I won't get in your way—but something tells me our dear friend Director Korbel doesn't have a few decades left in him.*"

Hilda, it seemed, already knew everything. Probably even Ayato's own internal conflict.

*"If it were me, though, I could have it done by tomorrow... Well, that might be a little optimistic, but soon, certainly. There's only one obvious solution available to you."*

"I could destroy her chains with the Ser Veresta..."

*"Dear me. You of all people ought to understand just how dangerous that would be. To begin with, you could have already done that long ago. And if you break the seal through brute force, who knows what kind of recoil will affect the target? In your case, it was only your full power that was sealed away, but in hers, she's sealed away her very life. I have to admit, I'm interested to see what the result would be, but I would advise you not to go down that path."*

"..." Ayato ground his teeth in frustration, unable to formulate a response.

*"Well, if you still don't like my proposal, I won't force you. I'll find another way to solve my own predicament. But are you okay with that?"*

"...I'll get back to you soon," Ayato answered reluctantly.

On the other side of the air-window, Hilda clapped her hands in delight. *"Wonderful! I look forward to your decision, Ayato Amagiri. Think it over well—for your sake and mine, and for your dear sister. Kee-hee-hee-hee!"* Hilda made a theatrical bow, and the air-window snapped shut.

Ayato was left hanging his head in silence, unable to so much as let out a sigh of defeat.

Hilda had seen through his feelings, through the reality of his situation, through practically everything. On top of that, she was already certain that he would choose her.

But if asked how he himself thought about it all...

"Ayato? Can I come in?" came Kotoha's voice from behind the sliding wooden door.

"Ah, of course. Please."

The panel slid open smoothly and precisely, but no sooner did

Kotoha see him than she tilted her head to one side in worry. "Oh my... Ayato, are you feeling all right?"

"Huh? No—I mean, yes. I'm just..."

She was remarkably perceptive.

"I know just the thing," she said with a light chuckle. "Ayato, why don't you take a bath?"

"Huh?"

"I've already prepared a change of clothes for you, and we've got plenty of towels. Nothing beats a nice, long bath when you want to relax!" She held the items all out to him with a beaming smile. "We've got a large open-air bath right outside the house. We normally let the students use it, but at this time of year, we keep it to ourselves, so you don't need to worry about anyone dropping in. And the water's drawn from a hot spring! Can you believe it?"

That did sound impressive.

He certainly was in need of a wash and a change of mood.

"In that case, I'd be happy to—"

"Here you go! Take your time!" she chimed, holding out the towel and fresh clothes.

Ayato made his way through the large building as Kotoha had instructed, when he realized that it was already eleven o'clock.

The year was almost over.

*This must be it,* Ayato thought as he came across a roofed passage leading out from the main building. It branched off farther ahead, no doubt leading to the dojos and student domiciles.

When he stepped inside, the space was much larger than he had imagined. The dressing room alone looked to be larger than even the guestroom where he was staying, resembling a public bath at an inn more than one at a private residence.

He didn't know how many students there were here, but there had to be several dozen at least if this was anything to judge by.

He stripped off his clothes and opened the inner door.

*This is...*

The bath, made from high-quality cypress, was large enough to accommodate twenty people at least.

Even the washing area was unusually spacious, again resembling that of an inn in scale. The open-air bath looked to be farther in.

For the time being, he set about wiping his body clean before taking a nice, quiet dip in the huge indoor bath.

Kotoha had said that the water was drawn from a hot spring, but it was completely clear and odorless, though comfortably soft to the touch. As his tense muscles began to relax, he realized that he had been holding in more stress than he had thought.

Most of that was undoubtedly mental stress.

He remained that way for a long while, before finally deciding to try out the open-air bath.

No sooner did he open the door than the cold, wintry air bit into his skin.

*Ugh, it's freezing...*

The open-air bath was built in a rustic design, surrounded by rocks and boulders, and even larger than the indoor one. Ayato waded through the water toward a huge boulder located in the center of it, leaning back and taking a deep breath. The temperature was somewhat cooler than that of the indoor bath, so there would be no problem taking his time to relax.

When he opened his eyes, he found that the clouds had entirely cleared, leaving only the myriad stars peering down at him.

Staring up at them, thoughts of his sister, of Magnum Opus, of his father, Masatsugu, and his mother too, all ran through his head, but he forced them out of mind.

All he wanted to do now was rest his mind and body.

Before long, his exhaustion began to finally catch up to him, and he found himself drifting off to sleep.

As he thought to begin making his way back to his room, he heard the door connecting to the indoor bath slide open, and he lifted his head.

Someone else must have just come in.

There was a small splashing sound.

Ripples flowed through the water, and at their source—

"K-Kirin...?"

"Huh...?"

Indeed, it was Kirin whose snow-white body shone brilliantly in the starlight, carrying not even a simple towel to hide her naked figure.

# CHAPTER 7
# WHAT COMES NEXT

"Kirin, I think that's enough for now."

"Huh? But I still haven't…"

Kirin was in the kitchen helping prepare for the New Year's festivities the following day, when Kotoha made her way in through the side entrance.

"Why don't we pick up where we left off a short while ago?"

"A short while ago? You mean…?" For a second, Kirin had no idea what her mother was talking about, but no sooner did she lay eyes upon her devious smile did she know. This was about Ayato. "R-right, Mom! What are you doing talking about us getting e-e-e-engaged?!"

"Relax, relax." Kotoha chuckled.

Kirin, all too aware that her face was turning red once more, tried to protest, but her mother merely took her by the shoulders and guided her toward the corner of the room.

"So how serious are you about him?" Kotoha whispered in her ear.

"What?!" Kirin blurted out, unable to move.

"I don't need to look very hard to see that you like him. That's why you brought him here, isn't it?"

"N-no! I was just…"

"Just…?"

It was happening all over again.

Whenever she spoke with her, Kirin always ended up getting caught up in her mother's peculiar way of doing things.

That wasn't to say that she disliked her approach. Kotoha was uniquely skilled in helping bring out the things that were buried deep in her heart—particularly those feelings that she, reserved and timid, couldn't give shape to.

"I just... I want to be Ayato's strength."

"In what way?" Kotoha asked as she stroked her daughter's hair.

"Ayato doesn't get along with his father very well... Even though they're both worried about the same things... At this rate, it isn't going to end well, and then..."

"I see."

"But I'm no more than an outsider; it's not my place to meddle... But I have to do something..."

"Hmm... In that case, why exactly do you want to be Ayato's strength? Because he's your friend?"

Faced with this question, Kirin found her mouth moving of its own accord. "Because he's an important person."

Of course, he was also a friend whom she had fought alongside.

He was the one who had come to her aid, who had shown her the way out.

And he was a swordsman worthy of her unreserved respect.

And yet—he was also important to her, in a way that went beyond all that.

"I see. That's what I wanted to hear," Kotoha said with a glowing smile. "So I guess I was right all along?"

"Huh?" Kirin looked up at her mother, blinking in surprise.

"There aren't many people whom you would describe in that way, are there?"

Kirin found herself unable to respond.

"Of course, in the end, the only thing that matters is how you yourself feel... But don't have any regrets, okay? You'll be fine. You have your own way of facing these challenges. And there's no way someone as cute and as charming as my Kirin could lose." With this, her mother gripped her on the shoulders once more, before turning her around and nudging her toward the corridor. "Let's call it a day. Why don't you go and take a bath?"

*

"Ugh… Why is Mom always like this?" Kirin muttered to herself, having, in the end, done exactly as Kotoha had suggested and gone straight to the bathing area.

Thanks to her mother, however, she had been able to put her thoughts in order.

Not only her thoughts, but the reasons underlying those thoughts, too.

She kept going over them all in her mind as she quickly undressed and made her way into the indoor bath.

She started by tipping a bucketful of water over her head, letting its refreshingly cool touch wash away her worries.

The bathhouse in the girls' dormitory at Seidoukan was somewhat larger than that of the Toudou residence, but it was all but impossible to have it all to oneself as she did now. She stretched out her legs, letting the warmth soak into her.

Only then did she truly feel as if she had returned home. There had been so much happening recently that she hadn't even realized just how much it was all affecting her.

"How long has it been since I used the open-air bath…?" she asked herself.

She normally only used the indoor bath but felt a sudden sense of nostalgia for the one outside.

She opened the door, letting the familiar ice cold air greet her as she made her way outside and stepped down into the water.

At that moment—

"K-Kirin…?"

"Huh…?"

She glanced up at the sound of the voice, only to see Ayato sitting wide-eyed ahead of her.

There was very little lighting in the open-air bath to begin with, but on top of that, he was sitting in the shadow of the boulder in the center of the pool, so it was little wonder she hadn't seen him until now.

"…"

They both remained motionless and silent for a long moment, seemingly experiencing a mental blank.

Ayato was staring at her naked body, while she was staring at his well-toned figure, when finally—

"Hyeeeeeeeee!" Kirin began to shriek, before quickly covering her mouth and squatting down in a panic as she tried to conceal herself.

"S-sorry!" Ayato blurted out at the exact same moment, quickly turning his back to her. "U-um… I'm really, truly sorry, Kirin! I didn't mean to…!"

"N-no…!" Kirin began, before sinking so deep into the water that it came up to her eyes.

Fortunately, Kirin had managed to stifle her voice before she could bring further attention to them both.

If someone had heard her and come running to investigate, the ensuing commotion would affect not only her but Ayato as well.

*This is…* She paused there, realizing what had happened.

"A-anyway, um, Ayato, did my mom say something to you?"

"A-ah, well… She said that only the family would be using it around now and that it was fine if I wanted to try it out, too…"

So she had been right.

Kirin slumped down, sapped of all strength, as she mentally cursed her mother. This situation was clearly her doing.

Perhaps she had been thinking of her daughter when she planned it, but no matter how you looked at it, this was going too far.

"I—I'm sorry, Ayato. This is probably…my mom's fault."

"What…?"

As she had expected, this revelation left Ayato lost for words.

Kirin, on the other hand, felt completely ashamed.

"I see… Anyway, I had better get out." Ayato's voice sounded somehow restless, but his tone had nonetheless returned to normal.

"R-right…," Kirin murmured, still not glancing up.

Of course. They couldn't afford to both stay here like this.

There was an audible gush of water and a rush of steam as Ayato stood up in front of her.

No doubt trying to avoid looking at her, Ayato went around to the other side of the boulder before stepping out of the bath, when—

"U-um, Ayato!" Rising to her feet so fast that she surprised even herself, Kirin reached out to grab his arm and stop him from leaving.

"Huh…?" Ayato stared back at her in astonishment, before once again quickly averting his gaze and covering his face with his free hand. "Wh-what are you doing, Kirin…?!"

"Argh…! I—I—I mean…!" Half-stunned by her own actions, she wasn't able to make her hand let go of his arm. She was so embarrassed that she wanted to do nothing more than run away and hide. And yet, she understood, vaguely, why she had done it.

Those were her true feelings shining through.

"…Um, Ayato." Her heart was beating so fast it felt like it might burst. Still unable to look at him directly, she felt her grip tightening. "W-won't you stay…just a little longer?"

"But what if—," Ayato began, before realization swept over him. He let out a deep breath, before stepping back from the edge and returning to the pool. "Ah… All right," he said softly.

Kirin felt a warm, gentle touch brush up against her back—the same touch that she had felt when they had both fallen in the ballast area beneath Asterisk.

"…Just so you know, I'm pretty embarrassed about this…"

"Th-thank you…," Kirin whispered in a weak voice, even more self-conscious than she had been back then.

But Ayato had responded to her request.

In that case, it was her turn now.

Or so she thought, but no suitable words or phrases came to mind.

So she remained silent, her mind all but going around in circles as she wracked her brain, trying to think of what she was supposed to do. What was she supposed to say? How was she supposed to say it? In the end, only one thing came to mind.

*    *    *

"I… I want to be your strength, Ayato."

Beneath the starry sky, in that world of white steam rising up from the water, Kirin's voice echoed softly.

"Huh…?"

Ayato had probably been expecting her to say something else.

It took him a short while before he could answer. "You've already helped me enough, Kirin."

That, on the other hand, was exactly as Kirin had anticipated.

It was a direct, calm, easygoing answer, the kind of gentle heartedness that Ayato had always showed her.

"…No I haven't."

It was true that Ayato had relied on Kirin in the past. Not only her, but Julis, Saya, and Claudia too—probably from as early as the Phoenix, when he had faced the twins from Jie Long (although, if it had been her at his side back then, she wasn't quite sure they would have won).

In any event, she was his friend, and he hers. It was only natural that friends helped one another and relied on each other's strength. There was something precious about that, something that went beyond words.

And now, she wanted what came next.

She wanted to support him—even the Ayato whom she had seen the previous day, clashing with his father, sulking like a child, letting himself be overcome by sentimentalism in that clearing from his childhood.

That was what family did. It was what her family had done for her.

And Ayato occupied a special place for her.

He was special, because he was him.

"…Ayato," Kirin began to slowly turn around, placing her arms around his in a soft embrace.

"K-Kirin?!"

As she had expected, her actions had left the young man overwhelmed.

She could feel his heart racing through his skin and was overcome with an indescribable sense of joy.

Of course, this had all left Kirin so embarrassed that she felt as if her own heart was about to melt. Skin touching skin, sweat mixing with sweat. Savoring this feeling, savoring Ayato's scent, she tightened her grip on his arms.

For her to be able to be support him in the way that she wanted, Ayato would have to occupy that special place for her.

At times like this, she always ended up comparing herself to others.

She didn't have the same kind of deep connection with him that came from being his fighting partner, as Julis did.

She didn't understand him to the same level as Saya, with whom he had spent his childhood, nor did she possess the kind of clarity or determination that Claudia had developed through her long suffering.

She was just his junior at school and hadn't even known him for two years.

And yet, still she felt this way.

No matter where she was headed, she wanted Ayato to be there by her side.

"...I'd like to be family with you." The words came out smoothly and without delay, her innermost feelings shining through.

"Family...," Ayato repeated in apparent confusion.

Right, family. Having come home, having spoken with her father and great-aunt, her mother and uncle, her feelings had finally taken form.

She placed her cheek against Ayato's back, closing her eyes.

"If we were family... I would be able to help you with your dad, we would be able to worry about Haruka together..."

Even if she couldn't intrude on his life as they were now, if they were family, surely she would be able to give him what he needed.

"We can support each other when we're lost... When you feel like crying, I'll brush away your tears..."

"Kirin..." He said no more than her name, but his voice was trembling.

In that case...if her words had managed to reach his heart, then there could be no greater happiness than what she felt right now.

"So... Ayato... Please..." As she spoke the words, she could feel her head growing hotter, her vision more blurred and distant. Her arms had lost all strength, her face leaning against his back drooping forward. "Please... Won't you... Marry me...?"

Even though her eyes were shut, she could feel her surroundings spinning around her.

"K-Kirin! Kirin!"

Then, Ayato's voice reaching her as if through a thick film, Kirin slipped into darkness.

\*

"Happy New Year!"

The next morning, the Toudou family gathered around the breakfast table dressed in their finest Japanese-style clothing.

Kouichirou, Seijirou, Yoshino, and Kotoha each wore formal kimonos, the men's ones decorated with the family crest and complete with divided *hakama*, and the women's embroidered with floral patterns around the dress. Ayato, being a guest, wore a plain *tsumugi* kimono with divided *hakama*.

And in front of him was Kirin, sitting behind dish upon dish of luxurious New Year's set meals, wearing a beautiful long-sleeved kimono.

However, her cheeks had turned scarlet the moment he had first greeted her this morning, and she still refused to meet his gaze.

*Well, I guess that's understandable...*

After all, after she had collapsed last night, he had wrapped her in a towel and took her to the only person he could be sure wouldn't misunderstand the situation—her mother—making sure to use his *shiki* technique along the way so that no one else could bump into them unawares.

Fortunately, Kotoha had agreed to keep it all a secret, but it had still no doubt left Kirin feeling incredibly awkward.

For Ayato, who hadn't known quite what to say in response to her confession, it was, in a way, good timing.

"Help yourself, Ayato Amagiri," Yoshino said, inviting him to begin.

"Thank you," he replied as he picked up a pair of chopsticks.

From what he had heard, it was Yoshino who had prepared the majority of the food. Every single dish smelled delicious, with the vinegar-soaked vegetables and fish looking especially superb.

"By the way, do you have any plans for today?" Yoshino asked him suddenly.

"Plans? Not in particular."

Yoshino broke into a wide grin. "I see, I see, that's good. In that case, I have a favor to ask of you."

"...Yes?"

Naturally, the dojo of the head branch of the Toudou family was much larger than that of the Amagiri Shinmei style's.

In the center of it, Ayato and Yoshino stood facing one another, wooden practice swords in hand. They were both still wearing their formal kimonos.

Dozens of students of the Toudou school sat alongside the walls, each of them wearing their martial arts uniforms. Among them, still in their formal garb, were Seijirou, Kouichirou, and, of course, Kirin.

"Um... What's going on?" Ayato asked uncertainly.

"What now? This little event is a kind of New Year's custom of ours. To put it simply, we have some representatives face each other so that the students can watch and learn."

"It's for the students...? I don't mind, I guess, but dressed like this?"

"This custom has a long history. It began when a former lord whom our family served was invited to a banquet on New Year's Day, and the head of the school at the time was murdered alongside him in all his finery. Since then, we've always done it like this."

"I see..."

It would, of course, be difficult for him to move dressed like this, Ayato thought, but at least he, with his divided *hakama*, would have the advantage. And yet—

"You don't need to worry about me. My clothes are custom-made to allow maximum mobility. Like this!"

"Wha—?!"

At that moment, she delivered a sharp thrust targeted right at his throat.

Ayato spun backward to dodge it, but Yoshino quickly followed through with a second, then a third attack.

If she could move this fast, he might have a problem.

"...I might not...know the Toudou style...but I can keep up with this, at least!"

Yoshino's swordsmanship was swift and direct, without even the slightest hesitation.

There were naturally similarities with Kirin's own particular technique, but whereas Kirin flowed gracefully from one move into the next, Yoshino's strikes were more austere and immediate.

"Don't hold back! Think of it as an exhibition match! I'm sure our students are dying to see the full potential of the famed Ayato Amagiri, champion of the Phoenix and the Gryps!"

"...In that case..."

There would be no need to hold back.

Yoshino was strong. The only other opponent he had faced around her age with that kind of skill and power was Bujinsai Yabuki.

She struck first from overhead, moving immediately into two consecutive sideways sweeps before stepping closer and—

*The Conjoined Cranes!*

If this had been Ayato's first time on the receiving end of the technique, he may very well have fallen victim to it then and there.

Thanks to the long hours he had spent training with Kirin over the past year, however, he knew how to react.

Moreover, Yoshino's technique wasn't quite as polished as Kirin's, leaving brief openings between each individual strike.

"Amagiri Shinmei Style, Middle Technique—*Twin Demon Hornets!*"

Ayato took advantage of one of those openings to launch a two-pronged counter, first thrusting forward to knock Yoshino's blade back, then pushing ahead once more toward her chest—stopping, of course, mere inches before he could make contact.

At that moment, a hushed whisper ran through the assembled crowd.

"He won so easily..."

"So that's the Amagiri Shinmei style..."

"No, it's not a question of style..."

At least half of the gathered students seemed completely struck with shock and wonder.

The majority of them were older than he was, and if they were living on the grounds, then they were undoubtedly serious about their swordsmanship. Ayato could all but feel their envy wafting across the large room.

They also seemed to be rather more disciplined, mentally and physically, than the students who had used to frequent Ayato's family dojo.

"Well now, it looks like I lost. That was quite something," Yoshino said, holding out her hand as she flashed him an unfeigned smile.

"I just got lucky," Ayato responded.

"There's no need to be so modest. We could do this a hundred times over, and I probably wouldn't even win once. Well, I might put up a harder fight if we changed the rules, but still, you're a tough one."

"The rules...?" Ayato repeated in confusion.

"Great-aunt usually wields a *naginata*, you see," Kirin answered for her as she rose to her feet.

"Oh, do you want a turn?" Yoshino asked.

"Yes." Kirin nodded, before changing places with the older woman. Her decorative long-sleeved kimono was nothing if not dazzling to the eye. "...A-Ayato..." Though first unable to meet his gaze, she glanced up to stare at him with determination. "If I win... will you give me your answer from last night?" Her face was as red as a fully ripened apple.

"...Ah, all right, Kirin." Ayato nodded firmly.

He wasn't so weak as to turn down her challenge.

"Then...let's go!"

Kirin was the first to make a move.

She stepped forward nimbly, tracing a flowing arc through the air with her blade as she began her assault.

Ayato braced himself, lowering his own blade to dodge the attack, but while he had expected her attack to fall downward into the now-empty space, she instead changed her sword's trajectory to direct it sideward in pursuit.

"Woah...!" Ayato dodged it by no more than a hair's breadth before leaping backward to put some distance between the two of them.

At that moment, he saw a flash of purple light run through her eyes.

"So that's your clairvoyance, then..."

Kirin's newfound ability, first awakened during the Gryps, allowed her to gauge a person's intended actions through the flow of their prana. It did, however, have its weaknesses. It wasn't as farseeing as Claudia's precognition, for instance; an opponent's intentions didn't always correspond to their actions; and even with knowledge of one's opponent's next moves, it was normally impossible to react immediately in the heat of battle.

Normally, that was.

The problem was that it was Kirin Toudou who had acquired that ability.

Already an extraordinary swordswoman, endowed with the fruits of years of unceasing work and effort, Kirin, with her earnest passions and determination, was, frankly speaking, anything but normal.

Indeed, out of all of Asterisk, probably only the Fairclough siblings were more proficient than her in the way of the sword.

However, they were both several years her senior. That advantage in years, in other words, amounted to an advantage in experience. Ayato couldn't even imagine what she would be like when she reached their age.

"But…are you okay, using that power?"

"Don't worry. I've been practicing, and I've asked Director Korbel to monitor it regularly. I'll be fine, so long as I don't overuse it."

Ayato breathed a sigh of relief. At least he didn't have to worry about that, then.

"…You shouldn't let down your guard!"

"That goes for you, too!"

The two of them lunged toward each other at the exact same moment.

Ayato thrust forward with his full strength, while Kirin, having adopted a similar posture, moved likewise. Their blades met head-on with a loud clap, before rebounding backward.

Kirin seemed to be ever so slightly taken aback.

She was also, however, the first to regain her posture.

Ayato's advantage lay in his raw power and speed, but Kirin was a step above when it came to movements and finesse. That alone was proof of the time and effort that she had devoted to her technique.

As she dodged low to the ground, Ayato leaped up high to dodge her, countering just as she began to lay into the pursuit, and giving her but an instant to scrape past under his blade and then meet the attack.

"Arghhhhh!"

"Nngh!"

Ayato deflected Kirin's downward strike, aiming to cut all the way from shoulder to waist, before spinning around in an attempt to knock her off her feet. Kirin, however, bent backward, letting it sweep right past her. Vivid lines of purple lightning flashed across her eyes before gradually fading away.

If he was being honest with himself, Ayato had to admit he was in a bit of a bind.

With his full power now freed from the seal that Haruka had

placed on him, he should have been able to easily overpower his opponent.

He might not have been able to match her in skill or technique, but if worse came to worst, he should have been able to gain the upper hand through brute force alone.

There was no doubting it was her clairvoyance that was preventing him from doing just that, but there was something else, too.

Kirin knew him intimately.

His sword techniques, his movements, his timing, breathing, movements—she knew his fighting style down to the very last detail.

Since the Phoenix, the two of them had trained with each other countless times over, enough for her to gain a full knowledge of what he would instinctively do in any given situation.

She had always had a good eye for such things and had probably even been able to pick up much of the Amagiri Shinmei style through observation alone. She probably understood his patterns of attack better than he himself did.

But in that case, he had the same advantage over her, too.

He probably wasn't any match for her in that regard, but he, too, had observed the Toudou style countless times over.

*In that case, she'll probably try…*

Just as the thought entered his mind, Kirin launched into a remarkably powerful flurry of attacks.

Ayato moved to meet the first one head-on, when she launched a second toward his neck before he even had a chance to catch his breath. If he managed to dodge that, next she would aim for his side, then his throat, his right arm, his throat again—

"It's the Conjoined Cranes…!" one of the students in the crowd gasped in excitement.

Kirin's version of the technique, however, was much more precise than Yoshino's. Ayato couldn't find even a single opening.

On top of that, her present application of the technique differed from her usual practice.

"Watch and learn, everyone," Ayato heard Yoshino call out.

"This will be the next stage of the Toudou style, after the Conjoined Cranes."

There were numerous traditional methods of countering the Conjoined Cranes—though they were all varying degrees of impossible to actually carry out. One could try to repel an opponent's blade through overwhelming force, or interrupt it through even more elaborate movements and techniques.

This time, however—

"Haaaaaaaaaaah!"

Ayato put all his strength into sweeping aside Kirin's overhead lunge—but she merely brushed his blade away, and then, with a flick of her wrist, came flying toward him.

He pulled back as quickly as he could, rotating his body and preparing to deliver a physical strike with his elbow—but as he had feared, Kirin's current form of the Conjoined Cranes had already accounted for his actions.

The Conjoined Cranes was so named because it looked, to the outside observer, like the folding of an origami crane. The intricate procedure was, however, nothing more than a sequence of consecutive attacks, and so to carry it out well, what was most important was fine control over one's breathing, timing, and senses, so that one could create a situation their opponent was unable to counter or resist.

Kirin's current form of the Conjoined Cranes seemed to be integrating his own attempts to counter into the sequence.

In other words, whenever he attempted to defend or attack, her response was immediate and incorporated directly into the chain.

"...Maybe we should call this the New Conjoined Cranes...," Yoshino, awe-struck, murmured under her breath.

If this was all thanks to her clairvoyance, then Kirin had gained an insurmountable advantage—one capable of turning the tables on a more powerful opponent.

It wasn't luck that she had defeated Xiaohui Wu. If the two of them were to have a rematch, she would, no doubt, run circles around his close-combat prowess.

"Ayato! Let's finish this!" Kirin called out as her movements suddenly sped up.

She was so fast that Ayato hardly even had time to respond.

But even so—

"I'm not going down so easily!"

The Conjoined Cranes wasn't, in general, the kind of technique that involved dealing a single, knockout blow. Rather, its goal was to chip away at one's opponent's defenses, until finally, a fatal breach revealed itself. In that regard, at least, this New Conjoined Cranes was no different.

In that case, he only needed to make sure that he wasn't worn down.

Kirin's blade flashed before him, Ayato racing to meet it and brush it aside, when once again she drove the pursuit—again, and again, and again.

Ayato had already memorized every technique used in the Conjoined Cranes. The current strike, a deep, rotating thrust from a low angle, was called the Laying Bait. Next came the Fisherman's Boat, then the Revelation, the Lovers, the Yatsuhashi, the Great Romantic, the Ocean Wavelets, the Kalavinka, the Sacred Lotus, the Warrior Kumagae, the Pinwheel, the Gathering Clouds, the Black Bamboo, the Path of Dreams, the Ninety Thousand Leagues, the Bleached Cloth, the Four Wings, the Sandalwood Lance, the Blue Waves, the Three-leaf Arrowhead, the Wings Abreast, the Calabash, the Water Wagtail, the Mitsudomoe, the Game of Hina Dolls, the Tripod Cauldron, the Parquet, the Citrus Blossom, the Mount Hourai, the Circlet of Flowers, the Clapper, the Blossom Crest, the Hundred Cranes, the Young Maiden, the One-of-Three, the Rose of Sharon, the Bank of Clouds, the Zhuangzi, the Nested Chick, the Kindred Twins, the Wind Orchid, the Sparrow of the Reeds, the Spring Dawn, the Gentian Wheel, the Anthill, the Desolated Field, the Rabbit-Ear Iris, the Gourd Vine, the Firebolt—

"She's doing all forty-nine moves...?!"

"All of them in conjunction?!"

"There's no way he can beat this..."

As the exchange drew on, the commotion bubbling among the students only fomented further.

Ayato could feel their ardor and excitement, but he wasn't about to allow it to interfere with his concentration.

He had to focus his attention solely on Kirin's movements, on responding to her blade and readying himself for the next strike.

To those watching, it must have looked like some kind of delicate performance.

Ayato, for his part, felt as if he was communicating directly with Kirin, albeit not in words. It was as if his hands simply knew, somehow, where next her blade would strike, and how next to repel it. They knew, too, that even the slightest mistake meant certain defeat.

He focused on the clanging of their wooden blades, on his fighting posture, and on the sweat trickling down his body. Whenever he leaped forward, he adjusted his movements so that he wouldn't slip or break through the floorboards, so that his speed wouldn't drop. The tip of Kirin's blade would come within a fraction of an inch of making contact before pulling away, leaving him practically no time whatsoever to tell his body to move. It wasn't a matter of one or the other anymore—his mind and body had become one.

The exchange felt as if it had lasted for ten, twenty, maybe even thirty minutes.

But that couldn't be right. It may have felt that way, but it couldn't have been.

The Conjoined Cranes excelled at driving its target to exhaustion, but its user, too, couldn't escape the same fate. Kirin had once said she was able to sustain the technique for around an hour, but Ayato doubted that she would be able to keep using this new form combined with her clairvoyance for the same amount of time.

"Nngh...!"

Her fatigue was beginning to show on her face, and while she had yet to make a mistake, her movements were beginning to become disordered.

The same thing applied to Ayato, however.

The winner would probably be whoever could hold out the longest.

He resolved to do exactly that, when there came an unexpected opportunity:

"—!"

"Agh…!"

The trajectory of Kirin's overhead slash was slightly irregular, giving Ayato a chance to repel it and move in to counter.

At that very moment, however, his battle stance fell apart.

"Arghhhhhhhhhh!"

"Hyaaaaaaaaaa!"

Kirin spun around, pulling her sword back up and then swinging downward, as Ayato, having fallen to his knees, raised his own blade one-handed in a desperate counter.

"That's enough!"

At that instant, Yoshino's voice rang out through the dojo, and the two of them finally relented.

Kirin's blade had stopped just short of Ayato's eyes, while his had almost reached her throat.

Silence fell over the hall, the students all watching breathlessly.

When Ayato's and Kirin's expressions both loosened, they each said, word for word and second for second:

"…You win."

# CHAPTER 8
# DETERMINATION

"What on earth could be so important that it couldn't wait until after New Year's?" Julis called out in annoyance as she opened the door to Saya's room in the girls' dormitory at Seidoukan Academy—before turning pale in alarm at what she saw.

Saya was sitting at a *kotatsu* in the center of the room, clinging to a heavy, padded kimono that she wore over her shoulders.

"We're sulking," she responded in an unusually sullen tone of voice.

That was one thing, but—

"You too, Claudia...?"

"Oh no, this is surprisingly comfortable." Claudia, sitting across from Saya and dressed in a similar padded kimono jacket, lay with the top half of her body slouched over the *kotatsu*.

"You've really loosened up since that brush with Galaxy..."

"There's still a rather severe issue left to deal with, so there's no cure like a good rest every now and then," she said with a carefree smile, before stifling a yawn.

"By the way, what happened to you?" Saya asked.

"Oh dear, look at your injuries," Claudia exclaimed. "Are those... burns?"

"Ah, this is just...well, it's no big deal. I was just training."

"You, who can resist your own abilities, got burned?" Claudia stared at her with skepticism in her eyes.

She may well have loosened up, but she was still as sharp as ever.

"Ah, I guess I'll join you both, then! I don't think I've ever sat at a *kotatsu* before!" Julis let out a light laugh, before sticking her legs under the blanket. "Oh!"

It was surprisingly warm and comfortable.

"Your upper body will get cold like that. Here, put this on." Saya, still lying down, reached into a large clothes chest and pulled out another padded kimono jacket.

"Uh… Are you sure…?"

"Is there a problem?"

"Not a problem, really, it's just…"

"Don't worry, Julis. They're surprisingly comfortable," Claudia said with a light laugh.

"…You're too fast to adopt new things."

"When in Rome, do as the Romans do, right?"

Saya began forcefully putting Julis's arms through the sleeves, giving Julis no choice but to submit.

"I suppose it *is* warm…," Julis had to admit. "I don't think it suits me very well, though."

"On that point, I think we're both jealous of just how good it looks on you, Saya." Claudia smiled.

"Heh-heh." Saya grinned, puffing out her chest as she lay down on the floor. "Of course. I'm always winning the prizes for best dressed and best dressed at a *kotatsu*."

"I don't really get what you're saying, but I suppose it does suit you…"

Saya, her padded kimono jacket, and the *kotatsu*—they were perfectly balanced, like the Holy Trinity.

"Well then, why don't you tell us what was so important that you had to call us both out now of all times?"

After all, Saya had summoned not only her, but Claudia as well.

Sure, Saya was probably lonely since her roommate had gone home for the holidays, but from the look of things, this went beyond just that.

"Like I said, I'm sulking."

"I know that! But why? I don't have a lot of free time, so if that's all it is, I've got other things to do!" Julis said with a heavy sigh, about to step away from the *kotatsu*, when Saya stopped her.

"Did you know that Ayato and Kirin went home?"

"What are you going on about? Of course I know—"

"And that Kirin went back to Ayato's house?"

"Wh-what?!" At this, Julis's whole body froze in place.

"And that she stayed the night there?"

"*What?!*"

Even from her position on the floor, Julis could hear Saya's teeth grinding in frustration.

"And that the next day, they both went to Kirin's house? And stayed the night there, too? They just sent me their excuses."

"—!" A sound that couldn't really be described as speech emerged painfully from Julis's throat.

She could feel the energy pour straight out of her body.

"I was shocked, too, when I heard," Claudia said with a bitter smile, her cheek pressing against the wooden tabletop of the *kotatsu*. "I had no idea that Kirin could be so daring... I wonder what's happened? First Sylvia, now this..." Her voice trailed off before she could finish.

"Wait, what did Sigrdrífa do?" Julis demanded.

"Unforgivable," Saya murmured.

"And here I was thinking we'd thrown ourselves into another heated battle..." Claudia's voice, for once, seemed to be laying bare her true feelings—turbid melancholy.

"What? I never...!" Julis, unable to stop herself from showing her anger, pulled herself further into the *kotatsu*.

She understood now—painfully—why exactly Saya wanted to sulk, but all that did was upset her further.

"Ugh, stop, Julis. If you crawl in too far—"

"You're lacking in refinement, Julis. The *kotatsu* is all about compromising with your neighbors."

"How can you say that when you keep pushing against my feet?!"

"Oh dear, this is most improper."

"You too, Claudia! You're hogging all that space for yourself!"

"Oh? You're as shrewd as ever, I see."

"Well now? What do we have here?"

"Ugh, Saya! Don't lift your feet like that! You're making it hotter!"

"Heh-heh-heh, this is just a technique to raise the temperature. Know ye the power of the best dressed at a *kotatsu*... Argh, too hot!"

"Two can play at this game!"

"Claudia, why you?!"

The three of them wrestled between the covers and the top of the *kotatsu*, until finally, with no clear champion having emerged, they each found themselves dozing off into a peaceful sleep.

*

"Phew..."

Only when he sat down on the balcony outside his guestroom—a cup of tea, which Kirin had brewed, in his hands—was Ayato able to feel at ease.

"Thank you, Ayato," Kirin, sitting down beside him, said with a relieved smile. "I'm sorry my great-aunt put you through all that."

"No, it was good experience. I should be thanking you."

"Thank you for saying that..."

It may have been mid winter, but the sun had come out and the wind had died down, so it was unseasonably warm—or rather, perhaps it was more that their bodies, still hot from the ferocity of their duel, couldn't yet feel the cold.

"Still... I couldn't beat you."

"Ah... The same goes for me too, though."

In the end, they had decided to call it a tie—although technically, it was Yoshino who had made the decision so that neither of them would have to admit defeat to the other. It was a face-saving measure for both the Toudou style and the Amagiri Shinmei style, but there was no denying that it had come at just the right time. Any longer, and Ayato didn't quite know what would have happened.

"No, it wouldn't have gone on so long if you had the Ser Veresta. You would have ended it right away."

"That's—," Ayato began, but he fell silent at the sight of Kirin's forced smile.

The way he saw it, it was precisely because he wasn't wielding the over sized Orga Lux that he had been able to respond to his opponent's incredible speed the way he had.

True, he could have tried to reshape the Ser Veresta to a more optimal form, but that still probably wouldn't have been enough. Even having regained his natural strength, he still wasn't particularly skilled at delicately manipulating his prana—and that had nothing to do with the seal Haruka had placed over him.

Now that the Gryps was over, according to Odhroerir's unofficial rankings, he was third in all of Asterisk behind Orphelia and Sylvia. Of course, that assessment was based on his performances wielding the Ser Veresta, so there was no denying that, in his current state, his actual potential had slipped somewhat.

"Heh-heh... You really are strong, Ayato," Kirin said, a touch of bitterness in her voice. "I guess it can't be helped this time, so I guess you don't need to answer right away... But I'll win next time, for sure."

"Kirin..."

He was glad to know how she felt toward him, but to be perfectly honest, he didn't have time right now to give her the attention that she deserved. Not until he had sorted out everything regarding Haruka, at least.

Of course, he also knew that he was, in a way, taking advantage of her feelings.

The same went for Saya's, too. He couldn't keep dragging it all out like this.

Which meant—

"I suppose, seeing as it *was* a draw, you do have the right to demand at least something from me."

"Huh?" Kirin squeaked, her face turning stiff.

She pulled her legs up from the balcony, before moving to kneel formally across from him.

"K-Kirin?"

"Ayato. I think you should face your father properly and tell him how you really feel."

At this, he found his body trembling ever so slightly. "That's… I mean, I'm already…"

"Then you need to try harder," Kirin bit back. Her hands, resting upon her knees, tightened visibly as she took in a deep breath and looked straight at him. "If I could do it, so can you!"

"—!"

The truth of that statement hit him right in the chest.

It was the kind of sincere honesty that he should have expected from her.

That was no doubt why he was able to answer as readily as he did: "…You're right. Okay, I will… You sounded a little like my sister just now, you know?"

"R-really? Sorry, I didn't mean to…," Kirin answered respectfully, waving her hands in embarrassment.

Both of them had returned to their usual selves.

"No, there's nothing to apologize for. I guess I can't keep patting you on the head, though, like an elder brother…"

"Huh?!" Kirin blurted out, averting her gaze. "Th-that's… D-don't change…" Her face had turned red all the way to her ears.

"Ha-ha, I'm just kidding," Ayato said with a warm chuckle as he moved to place his hand on her hair—before stopping so suddenly that not even he knew exactly why.

He had been able to do it so easily up until now, but this time, he hesitated.

"Huh? Ayato?"

He could feel his heart racing as Kirin tilted her head to glance up at him. "Ah, I…" But even so, he steadied his resolve as he began to slowly pat her on the head—more awkwardly than he remembered it ever having felt before.

Kirin, too, must have realized that as she stared up toward him, her lips curling in a warm grin. "Ayato... Are you blushing?"

\*

Ayato decided to head home again the next day.

Kirin, it seemed, wanted to stay at her own place for a while longer, but when he left, he heard her calling out after him: "You can do it!" That was enough to give him the strength that he needed.

"...I'm back."

Since he had called in advance, Masatsugu was waiting for him in the living room.

"..."

As Ayato stepped inside, his father merely glanced toward him, as silent as ever.

But that was fine. He hadn't come back to engage in idle chat.

Kirin had told him to face his father properly and tell him how he really felt. Of course, there was little chance that would turn into a lively conversation, nor was that his intention.

For Ayato, the best way he could think to approach it was to simply say what he needed to say, and hear what he needed to hear.

"I've decided, Dad—about what to do to help Haruka. I've thought it over."

"...I see..."

"I'm not asking you to change my mind. I just wanted to hear what you thought was best... Your real thoughts about it all." Ayato spoke softly, slowly, trying to keep his emotions from gushing up.

"..." His father, however, remained silent, arms folded.

Ayato, on the other hand, had decided to wait him out. He would be as patient as he needed to be.

At long last, his father spoke up: "...I suppose I don't deserve to be called a father. I don't have the slightest clue what I'm supposed to do, for you or Haruka." Masatsugu's tone of voice was as muted as Ayato's had been.

That wasn't the kind of answer Ayato had been hoping for, but he kept staring at his father, not once averting his gaze.

They remained that way for a long time, silent, until finally, dusk began to creep into the room.

All of a sudden, Masatsugu let out a deep sigh of resignation. "If I could, if it were up to me—there's nothing I'd like more than to hold Haruka in my arms again."

At this, Ayato's eyes snapped wide open.

His father's expression remained stern, but a crack in his voice finally gave shape to his inner turmoil and the truth that lay behind his words.

"…I see. Thank you," Ayato replied quietly as he stood up.

This was enough. For now, at least.

The atmosphere of the room, always so oppressive, felt somehow lighter.

He felt as if he had managed to pull open a window that had remained lodged shut for many years, finally allowing a breath of fresh air to blow inside.

"I'll bring her home with me next time."

"…I see."

That was the full extent of what passed between them before Ayato departed once more.

As he made his way to the bus stop along the twilight country road, he took his mobile from his pocket and summoned his desired contact.

Now that he thought about it, this was no doubt why she had called him the other day.

It was exactly as she had said.

No, as she had *foretold*:

"*Remember this, Ayato Amagiri. You will ask me for my help, sooner or later. I'm sure of it.*"

She had been right. There was no denying it. The prophecy was about to be fulfilled.

Just not, however, as she was expecting.

"*Kee-hee-hee-hee! I've been waiting to hear from you, Ayato*

*Amagiri.*" Hilda Jane Rowlands, alias Magnum Opus, appeared in the air-window in front of him. *"Seeing as you're calling me this time, I take it you've decided?"*

"…Yes. I want you to wake my sister."

A look of delight spread across Hilda's face as she flashed her sharp, devil-like teeth in a smirk. *"Wonderful…! A wise choice, Ayato Amagiri! So that means that you've accepted my conditions?"*

"Yes."

And by doing so, he was practically setting this savage beast loose on the world once more.

The responsibility for unleashing that creature rested with him. He was prepared to accept that.

But first—

"I also have some conditions."

*"Oh?"* Hilda paused, the whites of her upturned eyes peering down at him from behind her glasses. *"And what would they be?"*

First, he had to be sure that he could at least hold this creature back.

Ayato gave her a sharp look through the air-window as he carefully, cautiously, enumerated his requirements.

\*

"Kee-hee-hee-hee! Things are going to get a lot busier around here!" Hilda laughed delightedly to herself once the air-window snapped shut.

Ayato Amagiri had finally made the decision. Freedom would be hers once more—soon, she would once again be able to devote her every waking hour to her research and experiments. She glanced around at her laboratory deep inside Allekant Académie's research facility. Though now barren and empty, it too would soon finally be restored.

True, it all came with some rather meddlesome strings attached, but they were nothing she couldn't work around.

First, she would have to assemble her team and calibrate the mana accelerator.

As she was planning her next moves, however—

"You look like you're enjoying yourself, Hilda Jane Rowlands," came a cold voice, stripped of all emotion, calling out from behind her.

She turned around, her gaze falling on an unfamiliar woman standing in the corner of the room. "…And you are?"

It should have been impossible for anyone other than her to enter the lab. The vast majority of Tenorio's members wouldn't even bother trying, as Hilda could be guaranteed to deny them entry.

The woman wasn't wearing a uniform, nor did she have a school crest, so she probably wasn't a student.

Only when Hilda noticed that she was wearing a strange, mechanical necklace did she realize whom she was speaking to.

"Ah, I see, I see. So you're using a new body now… Varda, wasn't it?"

"Indeed, I am Varda. Varda-Vaos."

"Yes, yes. We met at that meeting, didn't we, the one with the funny name? Oh, I was so young and naive back then!"

At that time, she had still been a student at Allekant's middle school.

Even then, she had been in command of several research teams, and she had been considered a prodigy in meteoric engineering capable of standing alongside Ernesta Kühne.

"Well then, what business did you have with me? I'm afraid things have just gotten remarkably busy here, so I don't have time to stop and chat…"

"I'm interested in you. On a personal level."

"Oh? An Orga Lux like yourself, interested in a human like me? And here I was thinking you had already enlisted Ernesta Kühne?"

Hilda had known for a while now that Ernesta had established some kind of relationship with the Golden Bough Alliance.

That was no doubt the reason behind her frequent trips off campus.

"This has nothing to do with their plan. They might be making progress, but Madiath's way of doing things is too abstract, too lacking in rationality."

"Well, I suppose that's only natural."

Madiath Mesa *was* that kind of man.

"And Ernesta Kühne will always take the side of humans. Unlike you or me."

"That does sound like her."

Ernesta Kühne *was* that kind of woman.

"In other words... To put this in human terms, I'm still attached to Ecknardt's old plan."

Finally, Hilda's surprise and curiosity were piqued.

The Varda she had known had been more mechanical, less tainted by human emotion.

"But with Ecknardt gone, isn't that now untenable?"

Hilda had once lent her assistance to the Golden Bough Alliance. It had only been a short-term arrangement, brought to an end through a failure to reach consensus with her colleagues, but even so, intrigued by their current plans, she had continued to monitor them from a distance.

Which was how she knew that, at the present moment, they seemed to have reached an impasse.

"Our goal is similar to what you seek to accomplish. That being the case..."

"Unfortunately, I have no intention of cooperating with you ever again so long as you keep that underhanded fox around."

That should have gone without saying. Hilda still resented him for snatching away Orphelia.

"And what about our policy of mutual noninterference?"

"...Don't you want to know about Orphelia Landlufen?" Varda asked, abruptly changing the subject.

Hilda, however, often did that too, and so she thought little of it.

"There are several reasons why you haven't been able to replicate it."

"Oh?"

The conversation was finally getting interesting.

"The first is that you're dealing with a prime field. Orphelia Landlufen is a particularly rare, unique specimen."

"Yes, I've come to realize that, too—that she only turned out so well because of her latent potential. But I don't need to reproduce the results at quite that level. It would be enough simply to confirm my theory."

And yet, she hadn't been able to do even that much. In all her life, that had been her greatest humiliation and defeat.

Varda merely gave her a slight nod. "Exactly. Your theory is not incorrect."

"Then why?"

Varda pulled something out of her pocket, casting it toward her.

"Is this...manadite?"

It looked to be of high purity, but apart from that, there was nothing remarkable about it. It was the kind of specimen one could find in just about any research institute.

"The second reason why you haven't been able to replicate your experiment with Orphelia is this—the purity of your tools."

"My tools...?"

"That is a piece of a class-one grade Vertice Meteorite, freshly cut. You have no way of measuring it, but now that it has come into contact with the outside environment, it will have started to decay."

"Decay... I see. An intriguing hypothesis."

At the very least, none of the prevailing theories thus far in the field of meteoric engineering had posited such a process.

"What specifically is decaying? Artificial manadite might not be particularly long-lasting, but the purity of natural manadite doesn't change over time..."

"Not purity. Memory."

"...Come again?"

Hilda herself was often wont to jump between topics, but this Orga Lux looked to be even more erratic.

"Memory, you said?"

"*Of the other world.*"

"—!" At that moment, Hilda's eyes lit up. "I see! Yes, that's it! Yes! Kee-hee-hee-hee!"

"It will hold its form so long as it remains deep inside a dense meteorite, but once removed, the deterioration is swift. Those of extremely high purity, such as myself, are a rare exception."

"This is invaluable information, I must say." Even Hilda was possessed by a sense of duty and obligation—or so she liked to think.

She had her own distinctive way of showing that, however.

In any event, having been given inspiration that could lead to a significant breakthrough, she wouldn't be able to sleep easy unless she gave Varda something in return.

"I understand. If there's anything I can do for you, let me know. If it has to do with this matter of yours, I'll be pleased to help."

"That will do," Varda responded, before melting away into the shadows.

Of course, she hadn't disappeared exactly—rather, she had no doubt interfered with Hilda's sense of recognition. Varda herself might prove to be a specimen of great interest to her research, but now wasn't the time to be thinking about that.

"Kee-hee-hee-hee! Research beckons! But first things first! Once this little errand is over and done with, *then* it will be time to focus on matters of import!"

# EPILOGUE

Claudia, sitting at her desk in the student council room at Seidou-kan Academy, handed her a large case.

"In that case, Kirin, please take a look."

"Y-yes!" Kirin replied, lifting it open and picking up the activation body that lay inside. She took a long, careful breath, before switching it on, when the blade of a Japanese katana emerged out of the sheath.

It looked to be slightly longer than the Hiinamaru—perhaps around thirty-six inches in length.

Even when she had gone to perform the compatibility test, Kirin had felt a startling level of affinity with this katana-shaped Fudaraku.

"You had a compatibility rating of ninety-three percent, so the school has no objections about lending it to you."

In the end, Kirin had decided to accept the Orga Lux.

That was, in itself, a sign of her growing strength. The younger Kirin—even just a short time ago—would have wanted to wait and see before making a decision.

But things were different now.

On top of that, she could tell at first glance that this Orga Lux's ability was highly compatible with her own fighting style.

"Well then, why don't you try out?"

"Huh? H-here?"

"How about that sofa over there?" Claudia said with a wide grin as she pointed across the room toward the expensive-looking piece of furniture. "Please don't worry about damaging it."

Kirin hesitated in momentary confusion.

"It's okay. Please, go ahead. You already know the Fudaraku's ability."

"Y-yes. If you're sure..." Kirin, seeing no alternative, swung the blade downward toward her target.

And yet—

As a sudden jolt raced down her arms, the blade bounced right back up from the cushions.

"...It didn't even leave a scratch."

"Indeed. It has only just chosen you as its user, so it hasn't had much time to store energy. Right now, it's as blunt as a broomstick."

The Fudaraku's unique strengths lay in its ability to accumulate energy. In short, the longer it was stored in its sheath, the more energy it could accumulate from its user, which would then increase its power and sharpness. Since that ability came with its own burden, there were no other costs involved.

"According to our calculations, there's no limit to the amount of energy it can store. However, it does seem that it will become unmanageable after a certain amount of time, so you will probably first want to confirm its limit."

"I see..."

"I wouldn't be surprised if, in the hands of a swordswoman like yourself, you would be able to exchange blows with one of the Four Colored Runeswords after around a month."

"I understand. I'll look after it." Kirin deactivated the Orga Lux before placing it in the holder at her waist. On her left side was the Hiinamaru, and on her right the Fudaraku.

"Now you'll be able to stand head-to-head with Ayato's Ser Veresta," Claudia said with a soft chuckle.

"N-no, I still need to build up my strength before challenging him again..."

She may have been able to bring her duel against him to a draw the other day, but doing so had required her full strength. On top of that, Ayato had been at a disadvantage. It would be meaningless to fight him again before developing enough confidence in her ability to win.

"Speaking of which… Won't Ayato and Julis have made it there by now?"

"Ah yes, it *is* about time."

The two of them stared out of the window, their thoughts reaching out into the distance.

"Let's hope everything works out for the best," Claudia said, her voice soft.

"…Yes!" Kirin replied with a powerful nod.

\*

A month had passed since Ayato had requested Hilda's assistance in waking Haruka.

He had just arrived with Julis at the research facility in Geneva—a gargantuan installation equipped with the world's largest mana accelerator, a circular underground tunnel a little under nineteen miles in length.

"Kee-hee-hee-hee! Long time no see, Ayato Amagiri! I've been expecting you!" Hilda said in greeting as the two of them stepped down from their airship.

The snow flitting down from the overcast sky was exactly as he remembered these European winters—cold so strong as to freeze one's body to the bone. Hilda, however, was ecstatic, paying it no heed.

"And this would be…?"

"Julis-Alexia von Riessfeld." Julis's voice fumed with quiet, controlled rage.

Hilda merely tilted her head to one side, wearing an exaggerated look of confusion. "I see… And why are you here, exactly?"

"I'm accompanying Ayato. Is there a problem with that?" Julis stared back at her, her gaze so sharp that it could have skewered her right through.

"Hmm... Well, I guess it's fine. This way." Hilda paid her no further attention, simply turning around to guide them toward the facilities. Her dangerously unsteady gait was precisely as it had been a year ago.

"So that's Magnum Opus...," Julis spat out under her breath once they had fallen back a short distance. "I swear, I'd like to—"

"Calm down, Julis. Today's just about—"

"I know! But now that she's standing there in front of me... Because of her, because of what she did to Orphelia..." Julis pursed her lips so tightly that Ayato feared she would draw blood.

It pained him to think of the agony that this must be putting her through.

It was Julis herself who had wanted to accompany him here.

Ayato had promised her last year that he wouldn't accept Magnum Opus's assistance. She had agreed to forgive him for going back on his word but had insisted upon being there with him when the time came.

"I want to see her for myself," she had said.

Fortunately, there had been no problems when Ayato contacted Madiath to confirm this arrangement.

"But do you really think she'll honor her word?" Julis asked dubiously.

"Everything's being overseen by the IEFs, so it should be fine..."

In order to ensure that the tragedy that had befallen Orphelia could never happen again, Ayato had insisted on two conditions for rescinding the penalty that had been imposed on her:

Firstly, when using Level 5 facilities like the mana accelerator, she had to publicly disclose all information relating to her research.

Secondly, she had to acquire the full consent of all subjects involved in human testing.

He had actually wanted to prohibit her from engaging in human experimentation at all, but Hilda had refused to accept that. That wasn't entirely unexpected—it was her specialty, after all.

As such, he had at the very least wanted to impose certain limitations and obligations on her. That was his first condition.

His second condition wasn't entirely unrelated to the first. Those people who were subjected to human testing often found themselves forced into that situation due to circumstances outside of their control, and even when they didn't want to participate, they were often made to do so against their will. Like Orphelia had been.

Which was why Ayato insisted on seeing it all through for himself.

If Hilda ever violated those conditions, if she ever again engaged in such inhumane conduct—

"If that happens... I'll destroy this place myself." Ayato's voice was even colder than the landscape around them.

For the first time since they had arrived, Julis showed him a satisfied smile. "What a boneheaded idea! True, with the Ser Veresta there probably wouldn't be much stopping you, but that would be criminal, you know? *Very* criminal."

"I understand that. Anyway, so long as she knows I'm serious..."

Of course, he had no right to do such a thing, and as Julis had said, it would be a crime of the highest level. This mana accelerator had no doubt cost an astronomical sum of money to build and maintain, and it wasn't only Hilda who made use of it.

But even so, this was his way of taking responsibility.

He wouldn't allow another tragedy like what had befallen Orphelia to occur. No matter what.

"Well, I guess there's no helping it. I'll be there to give you a hand, when the time comes," she said, patting him on the back with a grin. "We'll burn this place to the ground."

"Julis..." Ayato couldn't be more grateful to hear her say that. His spirit lightened, he decided that now was as good a time as any to ask her something that had been on his mind for a while. "By the way...why are you always covered in injuries lately?"

Since the New Year, Julis seemed to be receiving new wounds and burns faster than he could count.

None of them were in any way major, and Genestella were, of course, fast to heal. And yet, it seemed that no sooner did one mend than another took its place.

"—! I'm… Well, I'm doing some intensive training, I guess."

"Intensive training? With whom…?"

"Uh-oh, look! We're going to get left behind if we don't hurry up!" Julis said, before increasing her pace and taking off in front of him.

*Well, if she doesn't want to talk about it, I can't force her.*

"Come now, this way," Hilda said, inviting Ayato and Julis into a large elevator.

She pressed some buttons on the air-window by the wall, when, with a low, rumbling sound, the elevator began to move.

"Now, I did mean to have all the preparations taken care of as quickly as possible, so you'll have to forgive me for making you wait this long. But I'm sure you understand. Experiments like this are most time-consuming. Something lasting only a few seconds can take dozens, even hundreds of hours of preparation." As she spoke, Hilda opened another air-window, before rotating it in their direction. "Now, I'll explain everything one more time. We'll use the accelerator to excite a sum of mana into a high-energy state, and then map that mana to the junction pattern of her ability to cancel it out. You can see a map of the facility here. This here is the injection point, and this here is the exposure point. I've already installed special equipment at the exposure point for your sister."

Hilda continued her explanation for what felt like several minutes, but Ayato couldn't quite grasp all of the technical concepts. The same must have applied to Julis, too, as she wore a look of obvious boredom.

At long last, the elevator came to a gradual stop, and the heavy doors slid open.

The sterile passage in front of them led straight to a gigantic control room, filled with raised voices and countless staff each dressed in the same type of white lab coat as Hilda, each busy at work doing one thing or another.

"Now, then…" As Hilda sat down in the main seat in the center of the room, a wall of air-windows and holographic keyboards appeared all around her.

One of those air-windows displayed Haruka's unconscious figure. She was lying inside a large device in a small room somewhere, as if she had been swallowed up by some kind of mechanical monster.

"...Hmm, everything looks to be in order," Hilda said as she looked over some figures and graphs. "We can start whenever you're ready."

Ayato was slightly taken aback by how quickly things were proceeding, but then again, he, too, had no desire to engage in needless talk. He gave her a brief nod.

"In that case," Hilda said with a click of her fingers, "let's begin!"

Almost at once, a flash of light lit up the air-window depicting the room that Haruka was in.

"Nngh...!" At the exact same moment, Julis bent forward, grasping her head in her hands.

"Julis!"

"Ah, highly sensitive Stregas and Dantes sometimes get a bit of a headache from the accelerated mana. Although we *are* supposed to be completely isolated from the accelerator in here... She must be very sensitive indeed. Don't worry, it won't be permanent," Hilda explained as she calmly looked back and forth at several of the air-windows. "More importantly, Ayato Amagiri, let me show you why exactly no one but me can do this. Watch and learn!" Her fingers danced atop the holographic keyboards that surrounded her. "See here, to cancel out an ability with a mana accelerator, you first need to analyze the target's junction pattern—which would normally take an extraordinary amount of time. Not for me, though. I'll do it in real time."

As Hilda spoke, the light engulfing Haruka began to gradually take the form of heavy, glowing chains.

"Adjusting the albedo like this not only uncovers the junction pattern but at the same time negates it. You could search the world over and never find anyone else capable of doing this! Only I've been able to master it! Kee-hee-hee-hee!" Hilda's burst of laughter was drunk with more than a touch of madness.

Even if he didn't understand what exactly she was doing, Ayato could sense for himself that what she said was true. For better or for worse, she was possessed of a rare talent.

The chains surrounding Haruka, though first all but transparent, gradually became more and more well-defined, until blinding cracks began to run down their surface—until they shattered in a brilliant flash of light.

"And... We're finished!" Hilda cried out. Her fingers, until now racing along the holographic keyboards as if playing a crescendo on a piano, came to a rest.

As silence engulfed the control room, Ayato leaned forward, staring into the air-window before him, when—

"Aya...to?"

Haruka's voice came out as a soft whisper as her eyes flitted open.

# AFTERWORD

Hi there, Yuu Miyazaki here.

As promised at the end of the last volume, this one was mainly about Kirin. The cover illustration might be of Haruka and Varda, but well, Kirin was given center stage there last time, and we've got to give everyone their turn! And, of course, this is the first time we've really gotten to see Varda, which is pretty exciting.

Now, I'd like to touch on what happens this time around. There will be spoilers here, so do take care if you haven't finished reading!

To be perfectly honest, this volume was probably the hardest for me to put together thus far. I already had a general outline before setting out to write it, but whenever I sat down to work, it was unexpectedly difficult to make Kirin step off the page and come alive. She's timid and reserved in character, tender-hearted and with an indomitable will, so I ended up wracking my brain trying to work out how she would convey her feelings. In the end, after trying a bunch of different scenarios, this was what I came up with. That said, while I did want her to take a step forward, maybe she's gone a little too far...

I've also finally been able to pull back the curtain a bit on Ayato's family, Haruka included. I had been holding back on revealing too much about them until now, but seeing how it all ties into the main events back in Asterisk, I thought it best to start shedding a bit of light on everything.

As mentioned above, okiura's wonderful cover illustration depicts Haruka and Varda! The same goes for the covers for the side-stories, but okiura's designs are about to enter new territory! I can't help but be struck by how awesome they are! The basic rule for the Phoenix arc in the first six volumes was to show just one character, while for the five volumes of the Gryps arc, we wanted to feature two characters on each one. We're going to be introducing a new format starting with Volume 12, so I hope you're all looking forward to it as much as I am!

Ningen's manga adaptation of *The Asterisk War* in *Comic Alive* is about to enter its final round! I'm so grateful to Ningen for really bringing the first three volumes to life so stylishly! I'd like to express my thanks for all the hard work!

Also, the final volume of Akane Shou's manga adaptation of *The Asterisk War: The Wings of Queenvale* in *Bessatsu Shōnen* magazine is scheduled to be released on September 10! It's truly a wonderful series, especially considering that the manga version is an original work, which we then worked on adapting into a pair of light novels! I've lost count of the times we both got so excited talking about everything over the phone. I'm so grateful! I hope you'll all join me and keep following Minato and all the other characters who are featured in it until the very end!

On top of all that, the anime adaptation of *The Asterisk War* has successfully reached the end of its twenty-four episode run! Now that a few days have passed since the last episode aired, I've had a bit of time to reflect on just how superbly everyone working on it managed to adapt everything to the screen! It's been quite a while since the project first got underway, but it feels like it's all passed in the blink of an eye. As the author of the original novels, I couldn't be happier! I hope one day we'll be able to bring Ayato and others back to the world of anime!

\*   \*   \*

On top of all that, I've been involved in supervising the setting for the mobile phone application *The Asterisk War: Brilliant Stella*, which is now available! Please take a look at it!

Last but not least, I'd like to express my thanks to everyone who's helped me out so much again this time around. Or rather, I'd like to apologize for always causing you all so much trouble once again.

I want to extend my deepest thanks to O, my new editor, along with my previous editors I and S for all their work organizing the anime and dealing with the rights. I'd also like thank everyone else in the editorial department, everyone involved in the anime, everyone who worked on the video game adaptation, and everyone else who's supported me along the way.

I hope to see you again in the next one!

*Yuu Miyazaki*
*July 2016*

# SEIDOUKAN ACADEMY

## SOUICHI SASAMIYA

Saya's father. Appears as a holograph after losing most of his body. Technical adviser for Seidoukan's Matériel Department.

## SILAS NORMAN

A former companion of Lester's. Attacked Ayato with Allekant's backing but was defeated. Now a member of Seidoukan's intelligence organization Shadowstar.

# ALLEKANT ACADÉMIE

## SHUUMA SAKON

Student council president of Allekant Académie.

## ERNESTA KÜHNE

Creator of Ardy and Rimcy.

## CAMILLA PARETO

Ernesta's research partner.

## ARDY (AR-D)—"ABSOLUTE REFUSAL" DEFENDED MODEL

Autonomous puppet. Fought alongside Rimcy during the Phoenix.

## RIMCY (RM-C)—"RUINOUS MIGHT" CANNON MODEL

Autonomous puppet. Fought alongside Ardy during the Phoenix.

## HILDA JANE ROWLANDS

One of the greatest geniuses in Allekant's history. Also known as the Great Scholar, Magnum Opus.

# characters

# LE WOLFE BLACK INSTITUTE

### DIRK EBERWEIN
Student council president of Le Wolfe Black Institute.

### KORONA KASHIMARU
Secretary to Le Wolfe's student council president.

### ORPHELIA LANDLUFEN
Two-time champion of the Lindvolus and the most powerful Strega in Asterisk.

### IRENE URZAIZ
Priscilla's elder sister. Under Dirk's control. Alias the Vampire Princess, Lamilexia.

### PRISCILLA URZAIZ
Irene's younger sister. A regenerative.

### WERNHER
A member of Chimulkin's Gold Eyes. Kidnapped Flora.

# JIE LONG SEVENTH INSTITUTE

### XINGLOU FAN
Jie Long's top-ranked fighter and student council president. Alias Immanent Heaven, Ban'yuu Tenra.

### XIAOHUI WU
Jie Long's second-ranked fighter and Xinglou Fan's top disciple.

### FUYUKA UMENOKOUJI
Jie Long's third-ranked fighter. Alias the Witch of Dharani.

## CECILY WONG

Hufeng Zhao's former tag partner, with whom she became a runner-up at the Phoenix.

## HUFENG ZHAO

An exceptional martial artist often entrusted with secretarial tasks by Xinglou Fan, who always gives him something to worry about.

## SHENYUN LI & SHENHUA LI

Twin brother and sister. Defeated by Ayato and Julis during the Phoenix.

## ALEMA SEIYNG

Jie Long's former number one, with overwhelming ability in martial arts.

 ## SAINT GALLARDWORTH ACADEMY

## ERNEST FAIRCLOUGH

Gallardworth's top-ranked fighter and student council president.

## LAETITIA BLANCHARD

Gallardworth's second-ranked fighter and student council vice president.

## PERCIVAL GARDNER

Gallardworth's fifth-ranked fighter and student council secretary.

## LIONEL KARSH

Gallardworth's student council treasurer. A member of Team Lancelot.

## KEVIN HOLST

Gallardworth's student council vice president. A member of Team Lancelot.

# characters

## NOELLE MESSMER

Gallardworth's seventh-ranked fighter. Alias the Witch of Holy Thorns, Perceforêt.

## ELLIOT FORSTER

Fought with Doroteo during the Phoenix, with whom he advanced to the semifinal.

 # QUEENVALE ACADEMY FOR YOUNG LADIES

## SYLVIA LYYNEHEYM

Queenvale's top-ranked fighter, student council president, and popular idol.

## MILUŠE

Rusalka's leader. Vocalist and lead guitarist.

## PÄIVI

Rusalka's drummer.

## MONICA

Rusalka's bassist.

## TUULIA

Rusalka's rhythm guitarist.

## MAHULENA

Rusalka's keyboardist.

## YUZUHI RENJOUJI

Studies the Amagiri Shinmei Style Archery Techniques. Acquainted with Ayato.

## MINATO WAKAMIYA

Leader of Team Kaguya. Alias Indomitable Perseverance, Kennin Fubatsu.

## PETRA KIVILEHTO

Chairwoman of Queenvale Academy for Young Ladies.

## VIOLET WEINBERG

Alias the Witch of Demolition, Overliezel.

## NEITHNEFER

Queenvale Academy for Young Ladies' second-ranked student. Alias the Goddess of Dance, Hathor.

## OTHERS

## HARUKA AMAGIRI

Ayato's elder sister. Her whereabouts had been unaccounted for, but she was discovered in a deep sleep, from which Ayato woke her using his wish for winning the Gryps.

## SAKURA AMAGIRI (AKARI YACHIGUSA)

Ayato's and Haruka's mother.

## MASATSUGU AMAGIRI

Ayato's and Haruka's father.

## ISABELLA ENFIELD

Claudia's mother. The top executive of the integrated enterprise foundation Galaxy.

## URSULA SVEND

Sylvia's teacher. Her body has been taken over by the Varda-Vaos.

## VARDA-VAOS

An Orga Lux capable of usurping the mind of its user. Currently in possession of Ursula's body.

# characters